THE MOSTLY MISERABLE LIFE
OF APRIL SINCLAIR

Love or Something Like It

LAURIE FRIEDMAN

darbycreek
MINNEAPOLIS

Darby Creek®
A division of Lerner Publishing Group, Inc.
241 First Avenue North
Minneapolis, MN 55401 USA

For reading levels and more information, look up this title at www.lernerbooks.com.

Main body text set in Janson Text LT Std 12/17.
Typeface provided by Linotype AG.

Library of Congress Cataloging-in-Publication Data

Friedman, Laurie B., 1964–
        Love or something like it / by Laurie Friedman.
            pages   cm. — (The mostly miserable life of April Sinclair ; #4)
        Summary: As summer approaches, April is conflicted about going to camp and missing time with new boyfriend Matt and her friend Sophie, who'll be visiting. Is her flame with Matt strong enough to survive a long absence?
        ISBN 978-1-4677-0928-6 (trade hard cover : alk. paper)
        ISBN 978-1-4677-0944-6 (ppk.)
        ISBN 978-1-4677-6190-1 (EB pdf)
        [1. Dating (Social customs)—Fiction. 2. Friendship—Fiction. 3. Family life—Fiction. 4. Camps—Fiction. 5. Diaries—Fiction.] I. Title.
PZ7.F89773Lov 2015
[Fic]—dc23   2014018570

Manufactured in the United States of America
1 – BP – 12/31/14

For my fabulous nieces and nephew,
Hannah, Mimi, Tillie, and Louis!
Love you all!

—Aunt Laurie

For I ne'er saw true beauty

till this night.

—*Romeo*

Sunday, March 9, 10:49 p.m.
Last night of spring break

I'm not a Shakespeare fan, but I love this quote because it's so romantic. When Romeo saw Juliet, he was captivated by her beauty. I'd like to think Matt felt the same way when he saw me tonight, but since I was sporting oversized pajama pants and an old Camp Silver Shores XL T-shirt, with a face full of zit cream, chances are pretty good he didn't.

I had just turned my light off when I heard a knock at my window. I got out of bed and pulled my curtain back, and Matt was on the other side. I couldn't believe what I was seeing. Part of me was happy he was there, but another part of me wished I could have rewritten the script and done a quick-change act before I opened the curtain. I hated that Matt caught me looking like such a mess.

"Come outside," he mouthed through the glass.

I said a silent apology to Mom as I discreetly used my curtain to wipe the zit cream off. No way was I letting Matt Parker see me with white goop all over my face.

As I opened the window, Matt put his finger to his lips for me to be extra quiet. I would have been anyway—if my parents had any idea I was climbing out my bedroom window in my pajamas, they would add it to the long list of things they've already told me I'm not allowed to do with Matt. He put his hand on my knee as I settled in next to him on my front porch. Even though the neighbors' view is mostly blocked by the two large pine trees in front of my house, I did a quick scan of my street to make sure no one was out and could see us.

"You look cute in your PJs," Matt whispered.

I glanced down at my flannel pants and faded T-shirt. Matt had on jeans and a T-shirt that showed off his biceps in this amazing way. I felt dumpy in comparison. "What are you doing here?" I whispered back. I tried to tuck some of the excess fabric of my pajama bottoms under my legs.

Matt grinned. His white teeth actually glistened in the moonlight. "I wanted to see you. Don't you want to see me?" he asked.

I nodded. "I just don't want my parents to hear us," I whispered. Even though my bedroom is the only one on the front side of the house by the front door, my parents and sisters are just across the hall.

I waited for Matt to say something, but he didn't. We sat side by side on my front porch, looking up at the moon and the stars. "So?" I said after the silence seemed to be taking a little longer than it should.

Matt threw my question back at me. "So?" he said. Then he added, "What are you thinking?"

I racked my brain to come up with what

I wanted to say. Since Matt came to see me, I thought he should be the one to talk first. But one thing I've learned about Matt since he moved in next door last year is that unless he has something he really wants to say, I seem to be the one who does most of the talking.

I decided to say what was really on my mind. "I think I look stupid in these pajamas."

Matt smiled and squeezed my knee. "I already told you I think you look cute." He raised an eyebrow at me, like he was waiting for me to move on to the next topic.

I took a deep breath. "I guess I'm kind of sad spring break is over."

Matt nodded like he wanted me to elaborate.

"You know, it was fun hanging out together, and I'm bummed that tomorrow we have to go back to school." I probably should have stopped talking at that point and just let it seem like my only issue was the fact that classes and home-work were less than twelve hours away, but Matt just sat there, looking at me, so I kept going.

"It'll be kind of weird to not be together," I said slowly. "You know, like, I'll be at the middle school and you're in high school, so we won't see each other all day." It was definitely Matt's turn to talk. He ran his fingers through his sandy hair like he was trying to think of something to say, but he didn't say anything. So I did. "I'll miss you," I added.

I wanted to reel the words back in as soon as they left my mouth. I couldn't believe I told Matt Parker I'll miss him. I sounded ridiculous.

Matt must have thought so too, because he broke his code of silence and started laughing. I was glad it was dark outside and he couldn't see me blushing. I shifted, partly because my butt hurt from sitting on the hard bricks but mainly because I was feeling like a complete and total idiot for telling Matt I'll miss him.

I think Matt could tell, because he did something totally cool and amazing. He lifted me up by my waist and pulled me onto his lap. I couldn't even believe it. One minute I was dying of embarrassment, and the next I was sitting on Matt Parker's lap. I could feel his thigh muscles tense beneath me.

"Well?" Matt asked as I settled into the

fold of his legs. His face was inches from mine. I could feel his breath when he exhaled. My stomach did a backflip.

"Well," I said back, mostly because I couldn't think of anything else to say.

"You know we live next door to each other, so we'll still see each other," he said softly.

"I know." I tried to shrug like it was no big deal.

Then Matt kissed me. Softly. On the lips. It was such a sweet kiss. His mouth lingered on mine for a long time, and when he pulled back he said, "This will be our place."

"My front porch?"

Matt's blue eyes twinkled. "Your front porch after dark."

The way he said it gave a whole new meaning to the bricks and mortar that have been just outside my bedroom window since the day I was born. "I like that idea," I told Matt.

He smiled a ridiculously cute smile. Then he lifted me as he stood and planted another kiss on my lips. "See ya." He waved as he walked toward his house.

I felt like Juliet as I watched my Romeo go back to his castle. Except I bet she wouldn't have been caught wearing baggy pajamas.

11:17 p.m.
Can't sleep

I'm wide awake. I don't know if it's because I'm still thinking about what just happened with Matt or because I'm wondering what's going to happen when I go to school tomorrow. I don't know what people are going to say when they find out Matt and I are going out.

It's not like it's a secret. But I didn't exactly post it online either. The thing is that Matt and I have a history, and in some people's opinions, not an entirely good one. Everyone knows he's the reason Billy and I broke up.

It's still hard for me not to think about what happened when he kissed me while Billy and I were going out, and how everyone freaked when they found out. Especially Billy and Brynn. I mean, Billy had good reason to be upset. Brynn too, but not as much. And no matter how many times I tried to explain things to her, she couldn't see anything from my perspective.

She just couldn't understand that sometimes things happen that aren't planned, and Matt Parker was one of those things.

I never planned to kiss him last fall. And when he kissed me, I hadn't expected to feel the way I did. Or that it would cause so much drama when everyone found out. When people realized that Matt and I weren't actually a thing, it finally blew over.

But now Matt and I *are* a thing. It's not that I'm embarrassed about it. He's so hot, and the four days we've been going out have made this maybe the best week of my life. It was just Matt and me, and no one else. And to be honest, I'm not looking forward to finding out what happens when other people get added into the mix.

The only people who know about us so far are my family, Sophie, Billy, and Brynn, and even their reactions have been mixed.

To be fair, Billy was cool when I told him. He actually gave me a hug and told me to "trust my judgment." He said it in a reassuring way, like he respected my choice.

Sophie was cool too. She was more than cool. When I told her, she screamed so loud into the phone, it sounded like she was right next to me and not thousands of miles away in New York.

Brynn was the total opposite. She was like, "Do you think that's a good idea?" I didn't think I should have to tell her I wouldn't be doing it if I didn't think it was a good idea. It bummed me out that Brynn couldn't be happy for me. We've definitely had our differences this year. But still, she's been my best friend since kindergarten, and it would've been nice if she could have been a little more excited for me.

My family's reaction wasn't much better. When Mom and Dad found out, they sat me down and gave me the Matt Parker Rule Book (Matt's name for all the stuff we're not allowed to do together). My sisters, who at seven and ten are too young to have an opinion about who I go out with, made it crystal clear that they like Billy more than Matt. Even my extended family—two aunts, two uncles, four cousins, my eighty-year-old grandmother, and her newlywed husband, Willy—have managed to weigh in on the topic.

Tonight at dinner at Gaga's, they grilled me about Matt and it was seriously annoying. I wish Sophie could have been here visiting Willy, her grandpa. Sophie, Gaga, and my cousin Amanda are the only ones who don't disapprove of my relationship. Why can't they all just trust my judgment knowing that I like him?

I like him a lot. I *more* than like him. I keep replaying the day I went to the beach with him earlier this week and how we kissed in the ocean and then he wrote the note on my arm asking me if I would go out with him. It was hands-down the best day of my life. Since it happened, it's what I've thought about every night as I've gone to sleep. And it's what I'm thinking about now, so I don't get why thoughts of other people keep creeping into my brain. But they are.

Why do I care what other people think? I don't. OK. Maybe I do, a little. Dad always says

when you start worrying about what other people think is when you have something to start
worrying about.

Seriously, April. Get a grip.

I don't care what you think about me.

I don't think about you at all.

—*Coco Chanel*

Monday, March 10, 7:22 a.m.
At the kitchen table
Eating funnel cakes
(For breakfast)
A bad sign

I have a bad feeling about this morning, and it's all because Dad made funnel cakes for breakfast. May reminded him it's what we ate when we went to the circus last year, which made me think, (a) Who serves circus food to their children for what is widely considered to be the most important meal of the day? And (b)

When everyone at school finds out I'm going out with Matt, will I be talked about like some freaky Big Top attraction?

One thing's for sure: I'm not ready to face the crowds.

8:52 p.m.

No one said anything. All day, during school, I kept waiting for it. I was sure that one minute, everything would be totally normal, kids going about their day, and in the next, there would be an information explosion. I pictured students at Faraway Middle examining bits and pieces of my story like shrapnel, and adding their own opinions to the mix.

As weird as that sounds, I think part of me might have preferred it like that. At least I would have known what people were thinking. But that's not what happened.

No one said a word about Matt and me. Were they just thinking things or saying stuff behind my back? I know it sounds like I'm paranoid, but when everyone found out I kissed Matt while I was going out with Billy, it was the only thing anyone was talking about.

I just don't want to be that thing again.

9:17 p.m.
Still thinking

I don't know why I'm hung up on this.

The only people who could have said something at school were Billy and Brynn. Since no one said anything, I don't think they did. The only other person who could say anything would be Matt.

He doesn't say much when he's with me, so I don't think he would to other people.

9:21 p.m.
Not taking any chances
Texting Matt

> Me: Have you told anybody?
> Matt: Told anybody what?
> Me: Oops!
> Me: Sorry! Meant for Brynn.

9:39 p.m.
Where is my brain?

I can't believe I just texted that to Matt.

I realized how dumb I sounded the minute he texted back, so I quickly made up the excuse about Brynn. It's been eighteen minutes and he hasn't texted back. It usually freaks me out when he doesn't text back.

But this time I'm glad he let it drop.

Tuesday, March 11, 1:43 p.m.
Study Hall
EVERYONE KNOWS!!!

I had a bad feeling when I got to school this morning that today would be the day, and I was right. At lunch, I was sitting with Emily, Kate, and Vanessa and we were talking about dance practice, which is starting up again at the high school after school today, when Julia Lozano came up to our table.

"April, I heard you're going out with Matt Parker! Is it true?"

Emily, Kate, and Vanessa all looked at me. Emily looked like she couldn't believe I hadn't told her. Kate looked like she wanted confirmation. And Vanessa looked like the salad she was eating went down the wrong pipe.

Everyone was staring at me. I wasn't sure if I was going to throw up or pass out. I said the first thing that came to mind. "Who told you?" It could only be one of two people.

"I can't say." Julia ran her fingers across her lips like they were zipped shut.

I had to know. "Was it Billy?"

Julia laughed. "God, no!" she said.

I had my answer.

6:45 p.m.
Home from dance
Crappy day

Kids are supposed to go to school to talk about things like algebraic equations, chemical elements, and verb tenses. But today, I was the only thing anyone was talking about. News of Matt and me was everywhere. People weren't just talking about me. They were talking to me. At least eight people (including Beth Schimberg, who almost never talks) asked me if it was true.

As I was walking into math class, Ashley Simon actually came up to me and said she was surprised to hear Matt and I are a thing. The way she said "thing" made it sound kind of dirty or dark. I wasn't sure how to respond.

Brynn has math with us and she heard Ashley. I shot her a be-a-good-best-friend-and-protect-me look. But the only thing Brynn did was ask Ashley where she got her skirt.

Even though I was kind of mad at Ashley, the person I was really mad at was Brynn. What made her think she has the right to tell everyone I'm going out with Matt?

When I passed Billy on the way from math to English, he actually asked me if I was OK, which I know was sweet, but it somehow made me feel worse. It meant he'd heard people talking about it too.

I could hardly get through the rest of my afternoon. And things weren't much better when I got to dance practice. During break, Matt and I were the only thing anyone wanted to talk about.

"I don't think you can trust him," Chloe said,

raising an eyebrow. I'm sure that was her way of reminding me that she'd sort-of liked him last fall, and he'd flirted with her, but it turned out he didn't really like her back. Or at least, that was how she saw it.

"Yeah," said Mya, one of Chloe's best friends. "We're in his grade, so we see him all the time." I wasn't sure what "seeing him all the time" had to do with anything, but Samantha, one of Chloe's other best friends, explained it.

"He's a flirt," she said.

All I wanted to do was change the subject. I didn't like thinking about Matt flirting with other girls. Plus, I'm the one he asked out.

"So what do you think of our competition schedule?" I said. Ms. Baumann had just told us that the District competition is early April, and then we have the Regional competition in early May, and if we qualify (which Ms. Baumann said we'd better!) we go to the State competition two weeks later. Thankfully, everyone seemed happy to talk about what's ahead of us this semester.

"We should definitely qualify," said Sara Feinberg.

Then everyone started jumping into the conversation and talking about which schools had strong teams. I was pleased with my topic-changing skills.

When practice was done, Emily asked if I wanted to walk home together and stop for smoothies. She's still not my favorite person, seeing as she's the one who shared all the details of my kiss with Matt last fall even after I swore her to secrecy. But we've kind of declared an unspoken truce, and I was glad to have the company.

"Matt's super cute," Emily said as we sat down with our banana smoothies.

I nodded as I sipped.

"I've always thought he was into you," she said. "I don't think you should listen to what anyone else has to say."

It was exactly what I wanted to hear.

Wednesday, March 12, 2:16 p.m.
English class

I should be working on a book review of *Ben Franklin's Almanac* right now. But how am

I supposed to focus on what happened in the eighteenth century when all I can think about is what happened in study hall? We had a substitute who just let us talk, so I decided it was as good a time as any to ask Brynn if she told people I was going out with Matt.

"Of course!" she said when I asked her.

I was shocked she admitted it so easily. I frowned at her. "Why would you do that?"

Brynn looked at me like I was one of those thousand-piece puzzles that are impossible to figure out. "I thought you'd be happy," she said defensively. "Every time we talk about Matt you tell me how great he is. I thought you'd want people to know."

Her answer made me mad. "Don't you think I should have been the one to tell people?"

Brynn shrugged. "Sorry."

But I didn't think she was sorry at all.

Thursday, March 13, 10:49 p.m.

I have evidence that ESP exists. I was lying in bed thinking that it's weird (not in a good way) to be back in school and not to have seen

Matt all week. I must have sent out a vibe or something because right when I was thinking it, he showed up at my window!

"Do you want to come outside?" he asked when I opened the window. I tried not to stare as he ran a hand through his hair. It was getting longer and it looked good on him.

"I better not," I whispered. I could hear sounds coming from the hallway which meant Mom and Dad weren't in bed yet. "My parents are still up. I don't want to get in trouble."

"I don't want you to get in trouble either," Matt smiled.

The way he said it was so cute. I tried to think of something adorable and clever to say, but Matt beat me to it. "Why don't you just stick your head out the window?" Then he grinned. "I don't think a head can get in trouble."

He had a point. He also had the most irresistible grin I've ever seen. I stuck my head out the window, and when I did, Matt put his hands on the sides of my face and then leaned in towards me and kissed the tip of my nose. Even though it was kind of awkward with most of my body still in my room, Matt Parker had just kissed my nose. My doughy, misshapen nose.

"I should go," said Matt when he finished.

"Yeah," I said like I agreed. But the truth is I wanted him to stay.

Friday, March 14, 7:45 p.m.
In my room
Not by choice
Very annoyed

I got sent to my room. I find it shocking that although I'm almost fourteen, my parents think it's age-appropriate to send me to my room. And the reason I was sent is literally so stupid, it's almost not worth writing about. But I have nothing else to do, so I will.

It all started because I was texting during dinner.

"April, are you texting at the table?" asked Dad.

Technically, I was texting under the table. But I didn't think that was the right answer.

Mom shook her head. "We have rules about that." Then she recited the list of rules and regulations that she and Dad made for how and when and where I'm allowed to use my phone.

I looked up from my phone. Everyone knows that an occasional broken rule (especially when it's one of many that never should have been made) is not the end of the world.

"Sorry," I said. "It was important."

"She's texting with Matt," said May, like that clearly did not qualify as important. "She and Matt are always texting."

"Yeah," said June, who I don't think even knows what a text is. "She and Matt are always texting."

Mom and Dad looked at each other and frowned like my sisters had just announced that I *always* do something really terrible like shoplift.

I could feel anger rising in me. "First of all, I'm not even texting with Matt. For your information, I'm texting with Sophie." I jammed my phone into June's face. "See," I said. "This text is to Sophie!" Then for whatever reason (and I think there were a couple of them, including but not limited to the fact that my parents are ridiculously controlling and that I was getting in trouble for something I wasn't even doing), I exploded.

"It's ridiculous that you and Dad have all these crazy rules about how and when I can use my phone. I'll be fourteen next month. FOURTEEN!" I said loudly. I knew my voice was too elevated, but I couldn't stop myself. "FOURTEEN," I said even louder. When I was done, I could feel little beads of sweat on my forehead.

No one at the table said a word. May and June looked at each other like they knew whatever was coming my way next wasn't going to be good.

Mom broke the silence. "April, texting so much is a waste of time."

"Having a device you can't use is too."

"April!"

I've never loved my name, but the way Dad said it made it sound worse than usual. He shook his head like he was disappointed. "You need to take some time and review your tone and attitude. And your room is the place you need to do that."

So that's where I am. And that's why, as I said, I'm annoyed.

Very annoyed.

I hate it when it snows on

my French toast.

—*Snoopy*

Wednesday, March 19, 6:02.p.m.
DAY 3

Today at dance, Emily asked me how things are going with Matt. I smiled and said things are great. But that's not the case. I haven't seen or heard from him since Sunday, which officially makes three days with no calls, no texts, and no moonlight make-out sessions.

Nothing! And I'm starting to freak out!

It's just so weird. Sunday afternoon I went over to his house, and we made popcorn and hung out on his couch watching this scary movie called *I Know What You Did Last Summer*. We had a blast watching it together. I kept screaming when scary stuff happened. Every time I screamed, Matt put his arm around me and pulled me in close to him. And every time he pulled me close, he stopped watching the movie and started kissing me. When the movie ended, he told me he'd seen the movie a bunch of times, but this time was his favorite.

Later that night, he showed up at my window, and we made out on my front porch for a long time. I thought everything was great, but now it's Wednesday and I haven't heard from him since, and I have just one question . . .

WHY?

Thursday, March 20, 10:54 p.m.
DAY 4

Now it's been FOUR DAYS since I've heard from Matt and I can't decide if I'm mad or desperate. I don't like using that word—it makes me sound like I'm stranded on a deserted island with no food or water. But I honestly don't get what's going on here. Everything was fine one minute, and now, it's like he forgot I even exist.

I'm giving this one more day. Then, I'm going to do something. I'm not sure what, but in the infamous words of Scarlett O'Hara . . . I'll think about that tomorrow.

Friday, March 21, 6:45 p.m.
DAY 5

OK. I said I was going to do something and I am.

When I went to dance practice, I made a cosmic deal with the universe that if I could just naturally bump into Matt and spend a few minutes talking and catching up, I'd forever have a happy, sunny disposition that would spill over positive stuff into the lives of everyone I ever come into contact with. Ever.

Honestly, I didn't think it was that much to ask for. Matt goes to school in the same building, so it wouldn't have been that hard to arrange. But the karma gods were not working in my favor this afternoon, which is why I'm now giving them a second chance. As I write this I'm sending out a prayer to the universe that Matt will call me.

Call me, Matt Parker. Call me.

8:45 p.m.

Taking real action

Matt hasn't called. I said I was going to do something about it, so I called Sophie and told her that I haven't heard from Matt since Sunday and it's freaking me out. One of my favorite things about Sophie is that since she doesn't live here, I feel like I can tell her things I couldn't tell anyone in Faraway.

"Call him," she said.

"It's not that simple," I said back.

"Yes it is," said Sophie. "If you want to talk to someone, call them."

I shook my head silently into the phone. "It doesn't work that way with boys."

Sophie laughed. "It works that way with anybody."

10:27 p.m.

OK. Maybe Sophie is partly right. If you

want to talk to someone, you should be able to call them, but I can't just call Matt. I'm going to text him.

10:42 p.m.

I texted Matt and he texted back, but it didn't make me feel much better. Our text exchange went something like this. (Actually, it went just like this.)

> Me: Hey!
> Me: What's up?
> Matt: Nothin much.
> Me: Where've you been all week?
> Matt (after 12 minutes): Spring training.
> Me: Cool.
> Me: How's baseball?
> Matt: Game tomorrow. Going to sleep.
> Me: Nighty nite :-)
> Matt: . . . (I think he must have already been asleep because he didn't text anything back.)

And he didn't explain why I haven't heard

from him all week. I mean, I get that he's busy with baseball. Whenever there's a show or something for dance, Ms. Baumann makes the team spend *all* our time at practice. Maybe Matt's baseball coach is the same way.

But still, what I don't understand is how during spring break, Matt seemed so into us, and now he seems like he's forgotten we're even going out. Something had to have happened, and the only thing I can think of is a little, tiny thing from Sunday night on my front porch.

I was sitting on Matt's lap and we were kissing. "I like these PJs," he said. I felt his fingers on the thin straps that crossed over my shoulder blades. I silently congratulated myself on ditching my oversized T for a fitted cami with a built-in bra.

Anyway, one minute Matt and I were kissing and his hands were on my upper back, then I felt them drop lower. I sucked in my breath as his fingers moved towards the sides of my rib cage. I kind of laughed and pulled away like it tickled, which it did, and we stopped kissing. Matt looked at me and opened his mouth like he was going to say something, but then he closed it again.

I don't think he was going to do anything. Plus, he knows I'm ticklish. So it seemed like a little, tiny thing to me. But maybe Matt didn't think it was so little or so tiny. What if it made him think that I thought he was going to go further and I didn't want him to? What if it made him think I'm the kind of girl who won't do more than kiss?

What if I am that kind of girl?

Saturday, March 22, 5:54 p.m.
Called Matt
Can't decide if it was a good or bad idea

I had a good reason to call Matt. I wanted to find out how his game went. I was calling to show interest, which is totally different from calling him because he hasn't called me.

When he answered, he said he was helping his mom bring in groceries and that he'd call me back. Then he didn't call back for almost thirty minutes. I don't see how groceries for two people could take half an hour to bring inside. At first, I was worried that maybe it was an excuse and he didn't want to talk to me, but the rational side of my brain knows that since it's just the two of them, he helps his mom a lot. When he finally did call back, I asked him about the game, and he told me every detail about the times he was at bat and what happened in the field too. He talked for a long time about baseball. He even explained to me how batting averages work.

Part of me thought I should just stick to talking about baseball. It seemed like he liked talking about it. But I had to know how he was feeling. It's all I've thought about all week. "So, it seems like you're not that into us," I blurted out.

There was an uncomfortable silence. "What do you mean?" he finally asked.

I hesitated. Part of me wished I hadn't started the conversation. "No big deal," I said, trying to sound like it wasn't. "It's just that I'm usually the one who texts first or calls. You know?"

"Um, not really," said Matt. He actually sounded confused. "It's not that I'm not into us. I'm just really into baseball," he added.

"Oh," I said, like that explained it.

But does it?

Sunday, March 23, 4:04 p.m.

T.G.F.F.

Thank God For Friends. Especially Brynn. It has been a long time since I've written something like that, but today, being with Brynn felt like old times.

Billy and I went to her house for lunch and our official countdown-to-camp meeting.

"This is an important summer," Brynn said as soon as we sat down with our sandwiches. "We'll finally be on the senior side!"

Then Billy started talking about all the things the ninth- and tenth-grade campers get to do that the younger campers don't, like how we'll even have our own beach. "This will be the best summer ever," he said.

But while he rambled on about midnight swimming, my mind drifted. I was thinking about Matt and if he really hasn't been around lately because he's been busy with baseball or if it's something else.

Then suddenly I started thinking about what will happen with Matt when I go to camp. I mean, how am I even going to tell him I'm going? It's not something we've ever talked about, and it's not like I can't go. This will be May's first summer there, plus I want to go. I love camp. And since Mom and Dad didn't let me go last summer, I've been looking forward to going back all year.

"Earth to April," Brynn waved a hand in front of my face. "Are you OK?" she asked.

"Yeah, yeah," I lied. I didn't want Brynn and Billy to know what I was really thinking about. I flashed a grin at them like I was just as excited about camp as they were, but Brynn wasn't fooled.

When we finished lunch and Billy and I were getting ready to leave, Brynn looped her arm through mine. "Can you stay and help me go through my T-shirts? I have way too many and I'll never be able to decide which ones to take this summer." She gave Billy an apologetic look. "Girl stuff," she said like that was his cue to leave.

"So?" she said when he was gone. "What's going on?" She had a concerned look on her face like she really wanted to know, so I told her how I didn't really see or hear from Matt all week and how he claimed it was because he was busy with baseball. "He can be such a mystery. It's like one minute he's in and the next he's out." I shrugged. "I can't figure him out."

I waited for Brynn to tell me she's always thought of Matt as a jerk, but her response surprised me.

"I'm sure he really has been busy with baseball," she said. Then she paused like she was thinking about what she wanted to say next. "I know I haven't always been that open to Matt. But if you like him . . . he must be a great guy."

I smiled at Brynn. It was awesome to hear her say that.

Brynn reached over beside her bed and picked up a magazine. "I saw this quiz called 'Are You Friends or Are You Dating?' Want to take it?"

I nodded. I guess it's better to know than to not know. So I lay down on Brynn's bed while she sat next to me and asked me twenty-five yes-or-no questions about my relationship with Matt. I imagined it was like being in a therapy session. I tried to answer the questions honestly. It was torture waiting while she tallied up the results.

I said a quick prayer. *Please God, let me fall into the you-are-dating category.*

When Brynn was done counting, she looked up at me and grinned. "You had seventeen yeses which means you're definitely dating!"

"What's the cutoff?" I asked.

Brynn waved her hand at me like that was irrelevant. "Who cares!" she said. "You have a boyfriend and he'd be crazy not to like you!" Then she stood up and started jumping on the bed. "You have a boyfriend!" she chanted.

"Thanks," I smiled up at Brynn. She stuck her hand out toward me like she wanted me up and jumping. I don't know if it was the relief of her acceptance of Matt or the goofy sight of both of us bouncing around on her bed, but I started laughing and Brynn did too.

And we couldn't stop for a long time.

Pooh, promise you won't forget about me, ever. Not even when I'm a hundred.

—*Christopher Robin*, The House
At Pooh Corner

Saturday, March 29, 10:44 p.m.
I need new clothes
Or a new family

Matt invited me to his baseball game today!!!
I'm so excited. It's the first real thing we've done together since we watched *I Know What You Did Last Summer* at his house, unless you count making out on my front porch as a real thing. I know Matt does. He showed up twice this week. The second time he came over, I pulled away while we were kissing. "Don't you think it's a little weird that all we've done together

lately is make out on my porch?" I asked.

Matt grunted like he didn't think it was weird at all. "This is our place," was his response. Then he pulled me into him, and we started kissing again.

I let it go, but it's been bothering me. Until today!

Matt asked me to come watch his game, and then we're going to get lunch and walk home together. I officially have no problems in life except what to wear! It's actually what I was trying to decide when May and June came into my room.

"Why are all your clothes on your bed?" asked May. Gilligan had followed them in, and he jumped onto my bed and settled into the pile. I shooed him off. I didn't want everything I own to smell like dog. I had something important to get ready for, so it wasn't great timing for May, June, and the dog to decide to hang out in my room.

But I was in a good mood, so I answered May. "I'm going on a date, and I have to find the right thing to wear."

"What do people actually do on dates?" June asked.

I was trying to decide how to explain the intricacies of love to a seven-year-old when Mom came into my room. When she saw me, she frowned. "Those shorts are way too short."

I met her frown with my own. As self-designated family seamstress and wannabe designer, Mom probably thought her opinion was valid, but I wasn't budging on it. "I'm wearing a long-sleeved shirt so it's balanced."

Mom shook her head like my explanation made no sense. "April, it's not summer yet. Your legs will be cold." June looked as confused as Mom. "If you have long sleeves on your arms, don't you need long pants on your legs too?" she asked.

"I think that top would look cuter with jeans," said May, who is in no position to give anyone else fashion advice. Her sense of style consists mainly of oversized athletic shorts, a worn out SpongeBob T-shirt, and the Mickey Mouse ears she bought last summer on our trip to Disney World.

"I agree," said Mom. "Why don't you put on jeans?"

But she didn't say it like a question. The last thing I wanted was for Mom to change her mind and not let me go to the game, so I put on jeans and made a mental note to never discuss clothing with anyone in my family.

Ever.

4:44 p.m.
Home from the game

The game was great, but it wasn't even close to the best part of the day.

I immediately found Matt on the field before the game. He looked super cute in his uniform, and it was cool how he looked up and did a head bob at me right when I got to the stands, like he was watching and waiting for me to show up. Once the game started, he was so intense and focused. It made me realize he really is totally into baseball.

But the best part of the day is what happened after the game. When Matt was finished, we went to get a burger at the stand across the street from the field. While we were waiting for our food, I asked Matt if he's always played first base, and that led to him telling me about all the teams he's been on since he played in Little League. It was fun picturing Matt as a little boy and hearing more about his childhood. He was in a really upbeat mood. We were talking and laughing. He even made a mustache out of french fries and let me take a picture him of him like that.

When we finished eating, Matt and I walked home together. The baseball field is on the opposite side of town from where we live, so it was kind of a long walk. As we walked, I was starting to feel a little self-conscious. Matt and I had fallen into one of our silences.

We were halfway home when we passed through Central Park, which is just the park in the middle of Faraway. It's probably the only thing our town has in common with New York (and I doubt it even compares). But it has some nice trees and places to sit. "Do you want to hang out in the park a little?" asked Matt.

"Sure," I said, relieved he'd finally said something.

I watched as Matt's eyes darted around the area, taking in the other people in the park. Then he led me to this spot inside a tight circle of oak trees. It was cool and shady, and I don't think anyone could see us through the trees.

He took my hand, and as we sat on the ground, he pulled me into his lap and started kissing me. It was exciting to think that we were in the park and that other people could be passing by but not see us. And kissing Matt in the park felt different from kissing him on my front porch.

His body was still warm from the game, and as we kissed, I put my hands around his neck. His tongue made its way slowly into my mouth. I felt Matt shudder as I wound my fingers into the hairs that had curled up at the base of his neck. He pulled me closer to him. I think it was his way of showing me how much he liked kissing me. I let my fingers slip lower, just inside the neckline of his jersey.

The next thing I knew, his lips were on the side of my neck. I wasn't sure what I should do. I didn't move as Matt gently kissed the side of my neck. I felt my body melting into his.

When he was done, Matt looked at me in his intense way. All I remember thinking was that his eyes were the bluest, most beautiful eyes I'd ever seen. Then our lips met again, and this time when we kissed, our tongues wound around each other. We kissed like that for a long time.

As we stood to leave, Matt did another scan of the area. I think he wanted to be double sure no one had seen us. I could hardly breathe. As we walked home, I was the quiet one for a change. It was like I was under a spell, a Matt Parker spell. Unfortunately it was broken the minute I got back. Mom met me at the door. "Did you have fun?" she asked.

But the way she looked at me made me feel like she wanted to know a whole lot more.

5:19 p.m.

I can't stop thinking about Matt.

Billy just called to say hi. It's crazy—the way I felt about Billy when we were going out was so different. He was like my best friend. I always had fun with him, but he didn't give me butterflies the way Matt does. Ugh! Did I really just use that phrase? I can't think of another way to describe it. And I literally can't stop thinking about Matt. It's like my brain is incapable of thinking about anything else. Even when I was talking to Billy, the only thing on my mind was . . . Matt.

I'm not sure what love is, but I think I'm in it.

You can have it all. You just can't have it all at the same time.

—Oprah Winfrey

Sunday, March 30, 2:04 p.m.
Back from lunch
OMG!

I should have said NO when Mom came into my room this morning and asked if I'd like to go for a special mother-daughter lunch. But in all fairness to myself, I would have had no way of knowing what she wanted to talk about. No offense to Chili's, but I'm not sure I'll ever go back after the seriously scarring conversation I had with Mom there. As soon as the waitress put down our platter of fajitas, Mom looked at me and said, "April, I'd like to talk to you as a woman, not as your mother."

I couldn't believe she'd actually said that. If I hadn't been so hungry, I would have gotten up and left. I should have.

"It looks like you and Matt are getting serious," said Mom. "Do you have any questions you'd like to ask me?"

Yes. One. *Can you stop talking and start eating?* But I didn't think I should ask it.

Things went downhill from there. "Are you just kissing?" asked Mom. "Or are you two trying other things? You know, Matt is older than you are." I don't think she meant for them to, but Mom's eyes actually drifted to my chest when she said it.

I shrunk backwards into the booth and stuffed a chip into my mouth. Did my mom seriously ask me that? "He's in ninth grade, Mom, not college," I said when I'd finished chewing.

"I know," she said. "I just want to be sure he's not trying to pressure you into doing things you're not ready for."

I shook my head like he wasn't. I couldn't

help thinking about the incident on my front porch, but it wasn't something I was about to bring up with Mom.

"I'm sure you and your friends talk about these sorts of things, but young girls don't always have accurate facts," Mom said without missing a beat. Then she paused. "April, you can come to me anytime you need information."

"Yeah, sure," I said, like I'd do that if I needed to. But what I really needed was for the waitress to bring the check.

Fast.

Thursday, April 3, 10:45 p.m.
Exhausted

I'm totally tired. All week, we've had extra-long dance practices so we're ready for the competition this Saturday. Plus, Matt came to my front porch Saturday, Sunday, and Monday nights. By Tuesday, it was actually starting to bother me.

I wasn't opposed to the fact that Matt was coming to see me. Since the day at the park, we've been having fun again like we did over spring break, and I guess he felt it too. But still, it seemed like all we ever do is make out.

So Tuesday night, I stopped kissing and started talking. I brought up topics I thought Matt would be interested in. I brought up baseball and school. I even asked him why his dog is named Matilda. I'd been wondering for a while. But when I asked him that, he didn't have much to say. I mean, he told me that he saw the movie when he was little and that he liked it. But he didn't tell me what it had to do with his dog.

I kind of have my own theory.

Matilda had special powers that helped her get rid of her evil parents. Given what Matt told me earlier this spring about his dad being abusive, and how he and his mom left when things got too bad, I thought maybe he named his dog Matilda because in some way he could relate. But that's just my idea.

Anyway, since that night, he hasn't called or texted, and it bothers me. I know if I said something, he'd say I'm being silly, that we go to school all day, then I have dance and he has baseball.

But still, it bothers me.

When I got to the high school for dress rehearsal, I ran into Matt. He was leaving the gym as I was walking in. He's always at the baseball field after school, so I almost never see him when I go to dance. We stopped and talked, and I showed him my costume for the competition.

He leaned toward me. "I bet it looks cute on you," he said.

I was about to say something flirty back when Ms. Baumann, who was on the other side of the gym, blew her whistle at me. "April, get dressed! You're here to dance, and you're holding us up," she yelled in my direction.

"She sounds like a bitch," Matt whispered.

"She can be," I said.

Matt did his head-bob thing. "You better go."

"Yeah," I mumbled like I agreed. But it was the first place I'd seen him all week, other than my front porch, and all I wanted to do was stay.

10:32 p.m.
In bed
For the second time tonight

I was so tired when I got home from dance. Ms. Baumann was in such a horrible mood today, and she made us go over our dances for tomorrow so many times. She kept looking at me like she was mad about what happened with Matt when I got to the gym. I asked Emily, who had seen the whole thing, if she thought that was why Ms. Baumann was acting the way she was.

Emily shook her head. "She was in a bathroom stall for our entire break," she said. "She either has diarrhea or tampon issues." I cracked up when she said that, and Ms. Baumann shot another look my way. I knew I had to be on my game for the rest of rehearsal. Which I was, and which is also why I was so tired and got in bed early tonight.

I was almost asleep when I heard the knock. I have to get up so early in the morning that I wasn't even sure I wanted to get out of bed, but I did. When I opened the window, Matt grinned. "What's up?" he asked as he helped me out of my room. His question irritated me. I didn't think I should have to remind him that I have the competition tomorrow. I crossed my arms across my chest. "I was sleeping."

Matt sucked in his breath like my response was too sharp. "Ouch!" He pouted and then made a face like a puppy that's been scolded. "Why the bad mood, California?"

One minute I'd been irritated, and the next I felt bad. How could I not when his face was all scrunched up as cutely as it was? Plus, he hasn't called me California in a while—the nickname he gave me the day he saw me sunbathing and squeezing lemons on my hair for highlights. He told me I smelled like the lemon trees back home.

"I'm sorry," I said. "I guess I'm just nervous about tomorrow."

Matt smiled and then ran a hand through his hair. He looked particularly cute when he did it. "Don't worry. You'll be great," he said. Then he started kissing me.

"Thanks," I mumbled between kisses. But I couldn't help thinking that I'd be even better if I got some sleep.

Saturday, April 5, 8:32 p.m.
In the bathtub
Where I plan to stay for a long time

Report on the dance team competition at Districts today: we did fine. Not our best performance, but not our worst either. Some people danced better than others. Unfortunately, I was in the *others* category. There were a lot of little things wrong with my performance. I could tell that my dancing was off, and it bothered me.

It clearly bothered Ms. Baumann, too, because as we were packing up to get back on the bus, she pulled me aside to talk. I felt my stomach churning as she started talking. A one-on-one with Ms. Baumann generally isn't a good thing.

"April, dance is about focus. Consistent focus. If you want to be good, you need to make dance your top priority." Ms. Baumann is taller than I am, and when she looked down at me I felt even smaller. I knew what she meant was if I want to be a good dancer, I need to get my head in the game and stop thinking about that boy I was flirting with in the gym the other day.

"Don't worry, Ms. Baumann, I'm totally into dance," I said.

But as I finished packing my bag to leave, I couldn't stop thinking about our talk. The truth is that I'm not totally into dance. I was when we first started. All I wanted to do was to make the team and improve. When I wasn't dancing, I was thinking about dancing. I wanted to be good, and I didn't even mind all the hours of practice. Even when I was going out with Billy, my main priority was dance. He used to complain that that's all I ever did.

But that's not what I care the most about anymore. I don't even like admitting this, but Matt is. It's not like I planned it that way, it just happened. Still, I feel like it's wrong in some way or it makes me less *me*. That thought was weighing me down as I got on the bus.

"What's up?" asked Emily as she sat down on the seat next to me. "I saw you talking to

Ms. Baumann. Is she pissed? Are you upset?"

"No," I lied. I didn't want to tell her what Ms. Baumann said or what was on my mind. Emily would totally get why I'm into Matt, but she's an amazing dancer and is always really into it. I bet she would say I should make both things my priority.

But it's like my brain will only let me think about Matt.

I literally think about him all the time. Just like I used to think about dance.

I don't get how a brain can be so into one thing one minute and so into something else the next. And the more I thought about it, the more it scared me because if my brain can be like that, so can other people's. And the other person I was thinking about was Matt.

Over spring break he was totally into me, but then when baseball season started, his focus shifted. Can a person really have two priorities at the same time?

Even if a person can be into two things at the same time, they definitely can't be two places at the same time. Thoughts of this summer crept into my brain. I couldn't help thinking what it will be like if my body is at camp but my brain is still in Faraway, with Matt Parker.

It takes courage to grow up and become

who you really are.

—*e.e. cummings*

Sunday, April 6, 7:54 p.m.
The real countdown begins—
To my 14th birthday!

I can't believe I'm turning fourteen in two weeks. At least it won't be hard to improve on last year's birthday debacle, when May and June utterly humiliated me in front of Matt the very first time I met him.

But if the suggestions I got tonight are any indication of how bad this year's celebration is going to be, I should hang it up and just stay thirteen. My whole family was at Gaga and

Willy's for dinner, and my birthday was the main topic of conversation. Everyone had opinions (even though I never asked for any) on how I should celebrate. Most of their suggestions left me without a response. Or at least, a response I could say out loud. "Why don't you have a scavenger hunt?" suggested my Aunt Lila.

"Or a *real* hunt," said my Uncle Drew.

As if either of those options was viable.

"How about a fishing party," said Uncle Dusty.

"You could have a Hello Kitty party!" said my cousin Charlotte.

Izzy agreed. "That's what we had, and it was super fun."

I broke my silence, but just to be nice to Charlotte and Izzy, who are only five. "I think I'm a little old for a Hello Kitty party," I said.

Izzy looked defeated when I said that, but not Charlotte. "You could have an Easter egg hunt," she said.

Izzy nodded like she liked that idea. "We love Easter egg hunts."

"Yeah, they're really fun," June chimed in.

"Yeah," I said, at least agreeing with them that Easter egg hunts are fun, which they are when you're five or seven, but not at fourteen.

My cousin Harry jumped in. "Why don't you NOT celebrate this year," he said. "For me, fourteen totally sucked."

"Harry!" his parents said at the same time. I wasn't sure if Aunt Lilly and Uncle Dusty were calling him out because he said *sucked* in front of Charlotte and Izzy or because they're on a campaign to try to get him to think more positively.

"How about a makeup party at the mall?" said Amanda.

I looked at her overly blackened eyes and bright scarlet lips. I was in sixth grade once too, but (a) I was never as into makeup as she is, and (b) even if I had been, my mom would never have let me out of the house like that.

"Would you like to have a knitting party?" asked Gaga. "You can invite a small group of friends over here, and I'd be happy to teach you all how to knit."

I paused for a beat before I responded. I

wanted Gaga to think I'd at least considered her idea. "No, thanks," I said.

"I know you think knitting is for old ladies," said Gaga. "But it's had a rebirth. Knitting is retro." I didn't reply. I guess Gaga interpreted my silence as stupidity. "April, do you know what retro means?"

I couldn't wait to leave.

9:02 p.m.
After age twelve, are birthdays always problematic?

I keep thinking about my birthday. Last year, all I wanted was a skating party. I wanted to be with all my friends, having fun. Brynn was even helping me plan it before Mom and Dad intervened and decided to throw the disastrous party they did for May and June and me.

This year, all I want is to do something with Matt on my birthday.

But I can't tell him that. Or anyone else for that matter. What am I supposed to do? Tell my family I don't care about celebrating my birthday with them? And what about Brynn? She's always been the one to help me plan my party. But she hasn't said anything about it this year. Not that I'm really expecting her to. I know we're getting a little old for the whole party planning routine. And even if she did, what would I say back? *Hey Brynn, the person I really want to spend my birthday with is Matt Parker.* I obviously can't say that.

Here's the thing. I do want to spend my birthday with Matt, but I don't want to have to tell him that's what I want. I just want him to instinctively get how much I would love it if that's what happened.

I mean . . . really . . . is that too much to ask?

Wednesday, April 9, 1:43 p.m.
Study hall

OK, Brynn brought up my birthday and what she said kind of surprised me. She just passed me a note that said: *Someone has a birthday coming up! Saturday at my house? We'll plan an awesome party!*

I hadn't expected her to plan anything, but after I read the note I smiled at her and nodded.

She smiled back and gave me a thumbs up like she totally had this one. I don't know what she has in mind, but the truth is that it felt good that Brynn still cares about my birthday, especially after everything we've been through this year.

Plus, Matt Parker hasn't said a word.

9:52 p.m.

I hadn't seen or heard from Matt all week, unless you count the time Monday night when I was outside in front of my house trying to teach June how to rollerblade and Matt waved from the car as he and his mom drove out of their driveway. So just now I decided to text him.

> Me: What's up?
> Matt: Going to bed.
> Matt: Tournament tomorrow.
> Me: Good luck.
> Matt: Thanks.

Well, I guess appreciation counts for something. Though frankly, not much.

Friday, April 11, 6:54 p.m.
Home from dance

Today at dance, Ms. Baumann reminded us that Regionals are May 3 and that it's super important because it's the qualifying competition for States. "Enjoy your weekend," she said. "Next week we're switching into high gear."

I was glad Ms. Baumann wasn't making us practice this weekend because I'm going to Brynn's on Saturday. I've been thinking it would be really cool to get her to help me plan a dance party. Matt hasn't said anything about my birthday, but if there's a party, he'd come. Plus, it would give me a reason to call him (which I kind of need) because he hasn't called me all week.

Two words: problem solved.

Saturday, April 12, 4:16 p.m.
Back from Brynn's

Planning didn't go like I'd planned.

When I brought up the idea of a dance party, Brynn completely shot it down. "I was thinking of something more low-key. Just girls.

Like a sleepover or something."

I took a breath and tried to keep my voice casual. "I was kind of was thinking more along the lines of a boy-girl party, you know?"

Brynn pursed her lips and looked down. "Oh. OK. I was just trying to think of something special," she said.

I knew I'd hurt her feelings. I felt like I owed her an explanation.

"I'd kind of like Matt to be part of the plan," I said. I concentrated on tucking a piece of stray hair behind my ear. "He knows my birthday is coming up, and he hasn't said anything." I could feel my face reddening as I admitted it.

"Oh, April," said Brynn. "Matt won't forget your birthday. I'm sure of it," she said, like she wanted me to be sure too. Then she reached over and gave me a big hug.

But she didn't say she'd plan a dance party.

7:43 p.m.

I just called Sophie and told her about my birthday dilemma. I know I'm being ridiculous. It's not even that I care so much about celebrating it. But I can't help that I want Matt to be part of it. I don't know why I bothered sharing any of this with Sophie. I should have anticipated her response. "Call Matt and tell him you want to celebrate your birthday with him," she said. "The worst he can say is no."

But in my opinion, that would be pretty bad.

10:48 p.m.

I was giving Matt until 10:45 to call before I call him. Now I feel like it's too late to call!

Sunday, April 13, 7:45 p.m.

When I woke up this morning, I decided not to call Matt. Asking him if he wants to celebrate my birthday with me just seemed like the kind of conversation you should have in person. So I walked Gilligan twice today, and the second time I did, I saw Matt. He was outside in his front yard, throwing a Frisbee to Matilda. When I saw him, my stomach felt like it was falling out of my body. Matt was shirtless and cuter than ever.

When he saw me, he waved in a super

friendly way. "What's up, California?" he said, like it hadn't been a week since I'd last seen him (with the exception of the car wave).

Looking at him made me hesitate before I responded. I didn't want to lead with either the do-you-want-to-celebrate-my-birthday-with-me question or the I-don't-like-that-we-go-days-without-talking-or-texting conversation. I feel like relationships should be more than a once-a-week sort of thing. But still, I didn't want to seem annoying. "Not much," I said lamely.

Matt ran a hand along his abs like he was checking them out. I'm not sure if he was even aware that he was doing it, but it was hard not to stare as he felt his own muscles.

As Matt started talking about the tournament he's been at since Thursday, my eyes drifted to the tan lines on his neck and arms from his baseball jersey. "It was Regionals," I heard him say. "And we won all our games, so we qualified for the state tournament."

Snap to it, April.

My mind flooded with relief as I made myself

focus on what Matt was saying about what the Faraway High baseball team has to do to become state champions. I know how hard the dance team has been preparing for Regionals and States. Matt is so committed to baseball. It totally explained why I haven't heard from him all week.

It made so much sense, it filled me with confidence. "So my birthday is next Sunday," I said bravely. I paused for a beat. I didn't want to seem too eager. "No big deal, but I was wondering if you want to do something."

Matt ran his hand over his mouth like he didn't like what was about to come out of it.

"April, I'm sorry but the state tournament is next weekend." He sounded genuinely disappointed. Then he flashed me his pearly white Matt Parker smile. "But hey, I'll be back Sunday night. Maybe we can do something then."

"Sure," I said in what I hoped sounded like I'd be fine either way. But as I walked home I couldn't help saying a little prayer.

Dear God, please let Matt's maybe turn into a definitely.

Lions, and tigers, and bears! Oh, my!

—*Dorothy*, The Wizard of Oz

Sunday, April 20, 7:45 p.m.
My fourteenth birthday

So far, being fourteen has been fine. It would be better if I was spending it with Matt. He said he would call when he was back from the tournament, but I haven't heard from him. When I got home from the diner, I walked past his house and it looked pretty lifeless. Maybe he's not home yet. I hope that's why he hasn't called.

Whatever.

I actually had a really nice day with my family. Dad closed the diner early for a late lunch celebration. Everyone in my family was there—Mom, Dad, May, June, Gaga, Willy, and all my aunts, uncles, and cousins. Even Dad's brother Marty drove in from Mobile with his son, Sam. Billy and Brynn were there too.

Dad made gumbo, fried shrimp, and french fries, and a huge chocolate birthday cake. It was a big improvement over last year's birthday pie idea.

Everyone brought me gifts, which was really sweet. Mom and Dad gave me a new phone, which I've been wanting, and I love it. Gaga knitted a sweater for me. Right when I took it out of the gift bag, I knew I loved it. "It's gorgeous!" I said to Gaga.

"It will bring out the green in your eyes," said Gaga.

"My eyes are hazel," I reminded her.

Gaga smiled. "That means brown with green flecks. When you put the sweater on, your flecks will stand out." I put it on and went to look in the mirror in the ladies' room, and saw that Gaga was right. My flecks have never looked better.

My cousins gave me some earrings and a necklace, which I put on immediately. "These look perfect with my sweater" I said.

Gaga winked at me. I know she must have arranged that.

My Uncle Marty gave me fifty dollars. I was shocked when he gave it to me. I think you could see it on my face, too.

"Daddy forgot to get you a present, so he gave you what was in his wallet," said Sam, who's five. Marty laughed and tried to shush Sam, looking embarrassed. But I didn't care. I was thrilled to get it.

I liked what Billy and Brynn gave me too.

Billy gave me a Saints T-shirt his parents brought back from New Orleans. "It's a re-gift," said Billy. "But it's never been worn, and I knew you'd like it. You can take it to camp." I grinned and gave him a hug. It was sweet of him to give it to me.

Brynn gave me a deluxe Bobbi Brown makeup set. It has everything you could ever want in it—shadows, blush, lip gloss, mascara, and a set of brushes. "I hope you like it," she said.

"Wow!" I was shocked. I couldn't believe she had given me such a nice gift. "I love it!" I told her. And I really appreciated that she had tried to plan a sleepover party for me. Brynn gave me a big hug. I'm taking it as a good sign that our friendship is returning to normal, which feels great. But what I didn't feel great about was how, after I opened my presents, everyone kept asking me questions about Matt and why he wasn't there.

"Where's your boyfriend?" asked Uncle Drew.

"Matt, right?" asked Uncle Dusty.

"We sure would love to meet him," said Aunt Lila.

"April's got a boyfriend?" asked Sam.

"April's got a boyfriend!" chanted Izzy and Charlotte together. I guess June thought it was funny because she started chanting with them, and then Sam got in on the action too.

"Is he still your boyfriend?" Amanda wanted to know.

"He probably dumped her and that's why he's not here," said Harry.

"He hasn't dumped me." I didn't like having to explain that he was at a baseball tournament and that I was going to see him later. Aunt Lilly actually asked me how much later and pointed out that it was already late afternoon. When she did that, the adults started shaking their heads and rolling their eyes, like they didn't think that me seeing Matt later was a good idea.

I didn't feel like telling them that it wasn't mine.

8:45 p.m.
Text from Matt

Matt: Happy birthday!

Me: :-)

Matt: On way back

Matt: Game went into extra innings

Matt: 2nd place by one run.

Me: Bummer!

Matt: Total.

Matt: Not sure about tonight.

Me: (Speechless.)

I didn't write what I was thinking, which was that getting that text from him was way more of a bummer for me than his baseball loss.

10:32 p.m.
My celebration continues
Sort of

Matt just left. As the rest of my family slept, we celebrated my fourteenth birthday on my front porch. To be honest, I can't decide if what just happened should be classified as celebratory. The first part was. I went to my window as soon as I heard the knock. I hadn't heard from Matt since his text. Part of me didn't think he was coming, but I still hoped he would. Matt took my hand and helped me out as soon as I opened the window.

"How's the birthday girl?" Matt said. But as he kissed me, he didn't smile like he usually does. His eyes looked tired or tense. Maybe both. "I like your shirt," he added before I could say anything.

I looked down at the Saints logo on the T-shirt Billy had given me earlier. "Thanks."

"I'm sorry about your game," I said.

Matt nodded like he appreciated it, but he looked away when I said it. I could tell he didn't want to talk about it.

"I've got something for you," he said as we both sat down. Matt reached behind him and produced a small box. When he placed it into my hands, I liked it already. "Open it," he said.

Slowly I lifted the lid off the box. There was a silver necklace inside with a little moon charm on it. "It reminds me of all the nights we've sat on your porch and looked at the moon."

I wouldn't have put it exactly like that. I don't really think we've spent much time looking at the moon. But I loved that he gave it to me.

"Do you like it?" Matt asked. Without waiting for my response, he lifted the necklace out of the box, unhooked the clasp, and fastened it around my neck.

I reached up and felt the cool silver of the charm at the base of my throat. It was hands down my favorite gift I'd gotten all day. "I love it," I said softly.

"I'm glad," said Matt. Then we started kissing.

Our tongues wound around each other, like that day in the park. I don't know if it was excitement over the gift or feeling older today, but something in me was feeling braver than usual. I think Matt could feel the difference too. I let him pull me closer. His fingers pressed into my waist. We were kissing even more intensely as his hands moved from my waist, up my back, to just below my shoulder blades. Everything felt so good and so right, being wrapped up in each other. It was just how I'd pictured celebrating my birthday.

Then I felt Matt's hands starting to separate. Slowly they made their way towards my ribcage. I could feel the tips of Matt's thumbs and fingers moving to the front of my shirt. I knew within nanoseconds they would be touching the Saints logo that covered my boobs. Matt's fingers pressed upwards into me. I tried to take a deep breath through my nose as we kissed. The last time Matt's fingers had ventured towards my chest, I thought maybe it was an accident. This didn't seem like one.

I pulled away. "Not yet, OK?" My voice didn't sound like my own.

Matt paused like he wasn't sure what to do next. "Yeah, sure. No worries," he said.

I smiled and went to kiss him again, but then he stood. "I better go," he said. "It's late."

I wasn't sure what to say. One minute, everything was great, and the next, completely awkward. "OK. Um, thanks for the necklace."

"Yeah, no problem." Matt did his head bob. "Happy birthday," he added. Then he left. After he was gone, I sat by myself on my front porch, looking up at the moon.

I had on the necklace Matt gave me and the T-shirt Billy gave me, and somehow, I'd never felt more alone.

I guess it's just my woman's
intuition. Every woman has one,
you know.

—*Nancy Drew*

Monday, April 21, 6:55 p.m.
Home from dance

I'm freaking out about what happened last night with Matt.

I thought Matt was trying to touch my boobs, but maybe he wasn't. What if that wasn't what he was trying to do, but when I stopped him, he realized that's what I thought he was doing, and that's why he left? Was he mad? Is he mad? What is he thinking?

Maybe I handled the whole thing completely wrong. Should I have just waited to see what Matt was going to do? What if he did try to touch my boobs? I know I don't want him to do that. But I didn't let him do it, and now it's all I can think about! I couldn't even focus in dance today. Thank God, Ms. Baumann didn't seem to notice. But Emily did.

"What's going on?" she asked at break.

I made up some lame excuse about having a big test tomorrow, and I think she bought it, which was good because there was NO WAY I was telling her (or anyone else for that matter) what's really on my mind.

8:59 p.m.

I'm so dumb.

I don't need to tell anybody what's on my mind. I need to talk to Matt. I need to just take a page out of the Sophie book and call him and tell him. That's what I'm going to do. He needs to know how I feel about things.

Dear God, please let this be a good idea.

9:35 p.m.

It wasn't a good idea. It was a great idea!

I just had the most amazing talk with Matt. I think we just took our relationship to a whole new level. I know that makes me sound like I've been watching too much Dr. Phil, but I'm so happy!

When I called him, I said, "I feel a little weird about what happened last night."

"Don't worry." His tone was softer than usual.

"I was really embarrassed," I said.

Matt laughed a little. "Me too," he admitted. He sounded relieved.

I hadn't even thought about what he was feeling. Then he said, "I guess I thought since it was your birthday and you're older, you might want to try something new."

I wasn't sure how to respond, but I didn't have to because Matt kept talking. "It's kind of like when you turn sixteen and you get to start driving a car." He paused. "But it's not just that."

"What is it?" I asked. I didn't want to push too hard, but I had to know what he was thinking.

I heard Matt let out a breath. "You're super cute."

"Yeah?" I said. I liked where this was going, and I wanted to hear more.

Matt made an "mm-hm" sound into the phone. "Kind of irresistible."

Wow. I couldn't believe Matt Parker had just used that word to describe me. "Kind of?" I said flirtatiously, even though I don't see myself as irresistible at all.

"Very." Matt was talking in a low voice, like what he was saying was for my ears only. "I really like you, April."

Even though he was next door in his room on his phone and I was at home on mine, I felt like we were right next to each other. I wanted to stop time and stay in that moment forever.

"I really like you too," I said quietly into the phone. "But I don't know if I'm ready for . . . *that*." I paused. I hoped he knew what I meant. "I guess that makes me sort of babyish." It came out like a statement, but it was a question and Matt knew it.

Matt laughed. "I still really like you." Then he had to go and we hung up.

I'm still not sure if Matt thinks I'm a baby

or not. Either way, I don't care. He said I'm irresistible.

Monday, April 28, 6:02 p.m.

Today at dance, Ms. Baumann reminded us that the competition to qualify for States is next Saturday and that we'll be working even harder this week than we worked last week.

"Impossible," grumbled Vanessa, who was sitting next to me while Ms. Baumann was talking. I don't see how it's possible either. It feels like all I did last week and over the weekend was dance.

"Girls, I will need your complete focus," said Ms. Baumann.

I sucked in my breath. It has been really hard to focus on dance lately. Especially since Matt and I had our talk. It's weird, but it's like everything changed when we talked, and even when I'm not with him, I think about what he said.

That makes it sound like I've been with him a lot. I haven't—I've been so busy with dance. But when we have been together, we've been super close. Like this weekend. We took Gilligan and

Matilda on a long walk. While we were walking, I kept brushing my non-leash-holding hand against his. A few times, Matt winked at me like he knew I was trying to get him to hold hands, but he didn't.

As we walked, I told him how nervous I am about the upcoming meet. "It's such a big deal to go to States. Ms. Baumann really wants us to qualify." I shrugged. "I guess I'm just scared. I don't want to let my team down."

When I said that, Matt picked up my hand and held it as we walked, like he didn't care who saw. Our neighbor, Mrs. Wallace, passed us and raised an eyebrow.

She might not have liked it, but I did!

Friday, May 2, 9:07 p.m.
Conflicted

Ms. Baumann canceled practice tonight. We had dress rehearsal yesterday, and she said she wanted us to rest tonight so we'd be fresh for tomorrow's competition. I asked Mom if Matt could come over after dinner and watch TV, and she said yes!

When he came over, I wanted to watch Survivor, because I know he likes that show, but May and June wanted us to play Monopoly with them. I was just about to say no way when Matt said, "Sure, I love Monopoly."

So we played, and it was actually fun. Matt was the banker, and he let June be his assistant. She's really into math these days, so he put her in charge of telling him how much change he should give back to people. Matt kept complimenting her on how fast she could add and subtract. He was sweet to May too. She bought a lot of hotels and houses and Matt nicknamed her Wall Street. She had no clue what that meant, but I could tell she liked it anyway.

Even though I would normally find it annoying that Mom and Dad kept coming in and out of the room to "see how it was going," they could see how sweet Matt was being to May and June. Thank God. My family loved Billy, and even though it's different because Billy and I had been friends before we were boyfriend and girlfriend, I guess I realized how important it is to me that my family likes Matt too.

When we finished playing, May and June turned on the TV and were watching *Sponge-Bob*. Matt and I sat down next to each other on the couch. Our pinkies hooked around each other. I didn't think my sisters were paying any attention.

"This was fun," said Matt.

"Yeah," I said. "Really fun."

Matt squeezed my baby finger with his. "It'll be cool this summer," he said. "When we're not so busy with school and baseball and dance, we'll have lots more time to just hang out."

I was just about to say how cool that would be when I saw May was staring at us. "April is going—"

"It's getting pretty late," I said, cutting her off before she could finish her sentence. I didn't want her to tell Matt I'm going to camp. I did a big pretend-yawn and stretch. "I have to get up super early for the competition." I walked him to the door and said bye. As I got into bed, all I could think about is how well everything went tonight with Matt.

It's almost like there are two of him. There's

the Matt who doesn't say much, who shows up on my front porch after dark, and doesn't always seem so into the idea of us. Then, there's the sweet, sensitive Matt who holds my hand while we walk and plays games with my sisters. It's weird. I never know which Matt I'm going to get. But I know I like the one I have right now who can't wait to hang out with me this summer.

How am I going to tell him I won't be able to do that because I'll be away at camp?

Suddenly . . . I'm not so sure I'm going to camp.

I used to be indecisive, but now

I am not quite sure.

—*Tommy Cooper*

Saturday, May 3, 5:48 p.m.
Home from Regionals

Today was such a great day! Our team did awesome at the competition and qualified for States, but the best part of the day was what happened on the bus on the way home. I was sitting next to Emily, and Matt texted to see how it went.

"That's so sweet!" said Emily when I showed her the text. "You're so lucky to have such a cool, cute boyfriend."

I grinned when she said it. I did feel lucky. I also felt like there's no way I can go to camp this summer. How could I go and leave Matt behind? I can't. Hanging out with him this summer will be so much fun.

Sunday, May 4, 9:03 a.m.
Decision made

When I woke up this morning, I kept my eyes closed and told myself I wouldn't open them until I'd made a decision about whether I'm staying home this summer or going to camp. I figured whichever option I pictured first would be the one I would go with.

Home it is.

5:03 p.m.
Back from Brynn's

Brynn texted me this morning that she wanted Billy and me to come over. She said she had a surprise. I was glad she wanted us to come over because I figured it would be the perfect time to tell them I decided I'm not going to camp. But when I got to Brynn's house, the surprise was that her mom had found a website with really cool camping stuff.

"I know how much camp means to the three of you," Brynn's mom said to us. "I told Brynn you can each pick something from the website and it's my treat."

"Isn't that sweet?" said Brynn.

"Thanks!" said Billy to Brynn's mom. "That's so nice." He scooted his chair next to Brynn's so he could get a better look at her laptop.

Brynn's mom looked at me. It was my turn to thank her, so I did. Then I scooted up next to Brynn too. But as we debated the merits of LED headlamps, Nalgene water bottles, and personalized stationary, I knew making that decision would be simple compared to telling my friends and family that I wouldn't be going to camp.

Thursday, May 8, 6:45 p.m.
Dance practice for States officially begins

Rehearsal for States kicked into high gear today. Ms. Baumann gave us a long lecture on being in sync with each other. "It's all about timing," she said. "If one dancer is off, the dance doesn't work."

As she talked, I tried to focus on the importance of timing in dance, but I kept thinking about camp and why I haven't told my parents and Brynn and Billy that I don't want to go. It's because I haven't found the right moment.

As Ms. Baumann said, it's all about timing.

Friday, May 9, 1:47 p.m.
Study hall

Brynn just asked me if I wanted to come over on Saturday to plan what we're taking to camp. I didn't tell her I don't need to plan what I'm taking if I'm not going. "I can't come," I said. "I have dance practice."

She shook her head like I needed to get my priorities straight. "I invited Billy too."

It seemed weird that she'd include Billy in this plan. "Why would you invite him?" I asked. "He doesn't care what he takes to camp."

"He's coming," she said, like I was wrong to assume he didn't care. Then it dawned on me that Saturday would be the perfect time to tell them I'm not going to camp. "I finish practice at two. Could we do it then?"

"Sure," said Brynn like two o'clock was no problem.

Saturday, May 10, 4:42 p.m.
Home from Brynn's
Conflicted

OK. I'm completely conflicted over what to do about camp.

I got to Brynn's house today right after practice, and when I got there, she and Billy were on her bed with her computer open. When I walked into her room, Brynn closed her computer like she didn't want me to see whatever she and Billy were looking at. I felt like an intruder.

"Are you guys planning what you're taking to camp?" I asked.

"We're watching an episode of *Survivor*," said Billy. Then he looked at Brynn. "Why did you close the computer? We only have ten minutes left."

Brynn looked guilty.

"You can finish," I said.

Brynn opened her computer and I sat at her desk while she and Billy finished the episode.

I sat there pretending like it didn't bother me, but it did.

First of all, Brynn knows I love *Survivor.* She could have waited and watched it when I got there. And I had told her I could come at two, so she must have invited Billy over earlier. And if they were almost done with the episode, he must have come a lot earlier.

As I sat there watching them watch *Survivor* together, I got more and more conflicted about what I'm going to do this summer. I don't want them to go to camp without me. They'll be inseparable, and I'll spend another summer wondering what's going on with them while I'm not around.

I definitely don't want that.

10:55 p.m.
Decision made

Matt came over tonight and we sat on the couch and watched a movie. It was kind of like a date, but at home. It was really fun because we were watching a horror movie and no one else in my family wanted to watch it, so it was just the two of us. At this one super scary part, I leaned into Matt like I was scared. He put his arm around me and pulled me in next to him. I thought he was going to let go when the scary part was over, but he didn't. We sat on my couch, with his arm looped around me. When we heard footsteps coming our way, Matt moved his arm, scooted forward and sat up straight on the edge of the couch.

Mom stuck her head in the family room. "Just checking on you," she said in a too-parental way.

"Everything's fine, Mrs. Sinclair," Matt said in his most polite voice.

When Mom left, Matt sunk back into the couch and we grinned at each other in a conspiratorial way, and then he wrapped his arm around me again. It wasn't a big deal, but it made me feel super close to him. When the movie was over, I walked outside with Matt. We were standing under an oak tree in my front yard, and Matt put both arms around me and kissed me full on the lips. I thought about how Mrs. Wallace saw us holding hands. Most of me hoped no one could see us now, but part of me didn't care.

"Fun night," Matt whispered.

I couldn't help thinking that there would be lots more of them this summer.

Two roads diverged in a wood, and I—

I took the one less traveled by.

—Robert Frost

Sunday, May 11, 10:04 a.m.
How to ruin a plate of perfectly good
pancakes

Tell your parents you don't want to go to camp. That's what I did at breakfast, and you would have thought I said I wanted to sell one of my sisters.

"April, why in the world would you not want to go to camp?" asked Dad.

"Why would you not want to go to camp?" The way Mom repeated the question made her sound like June. And the worst part was that it was a rhetorical question. They knew why I didn't want to go. "Is it about that boy?" asked Mom.

I pushed my pancakes away. "His name is Matt."

"You're going to camp," said Dad, like the discussion was over.

But I wasn't done. "How can you make me go to camp this summer when I don't want to go and you wouldn't let me go last summer when I did want to go?" Even a young child with a low IQ could understand the lack of fairness there. "I'm fourteen. I should get to make some of my own decisions, like what I do over the summer."

Dad looked at Mom. I could tell he thought I'd made a good point.

"April, I don't think spending the whole summer at home and hanging out with Matt is . . ." Dad paused like he was trying to figure out what to say. ". . . a good idea. But I do respect the fact that you're a teenager, and you should get to make decisions about what you do with your life."

I couldn't believe what I was hearing.

Actually, Dad didn't look like he believed what he was saying either. I wanted to do a victory dance, but Dad wasn't done talking. "You can decide what you want to do, but I ask that you think about it carefully." He reminded me how much I love camp and that this is my next to last summer to go.

Then Mom gestured toward May, who was sitting next to her. "Don't forget this is your sister's first time to go to camp." Mom knew I didn't need reminding about this. It's the only thing May has talked about for the last two weeks.

When I looked at May, she looked down at her pancakes. Even though I hadn't eaten much, I felt nauseous. "I know May will be disappointed if you're not there," Mom added, like she was my sister's spokesperson.

May looked up at me. I knew how disappointed she'd be if I didn't go.

Dad rubbed his chin, like he wanted his last point to be a good one. "April, camp is only four weeks, which means you'd still have plenty of time over the summer to spend with Matt."

May looked up at me. I could tell she was

trying to say a lot without saying a word.

"I'll think it over," I mumbled.

Even though my parents can be annoying and unreasonable, they weren't being either about this, which for some strange reason I found to be very unsettling.

10:17 a.m.

A crying sister doesn't help

May just came into my room with big tears in her eyes. "I heard what you said."

Of course she'd heard what I said, she was sitting right across the table from me at breakfast when I said it. But I knew what she meant. I pulled her up next to me on my bed. "Don't worry," I said. "You'll have an amazing time at camp whether I'm there or not."

She rested her head on my shoulder. "I'll have a more amazing time if you're there."

It was sweet hearing that, but it definitely wasn't making my decision any easier.

Wednesday, May 14, 10:32 p.m.

Matt came over a few minutes ago, and we

made out on my front porch. This is going to sound weird, but I'd been thinking about kissing him ever since I'd walked Gilligan earlier.

Mom asked me if I'd take him out before dinner, and when I did, Matt was outside. He'd just finished a run. He looked so boyish and hot, all shirtless and sweaty. "I was thinking about you today," he said as I fell into step beside him.

I bit my lip to try to keep from grinning.

"You look cute when you do that," he said.

"I do?" I asked in what I think was a pretty cute, flirtatious way.

Matt must have thought so too. "It makes me want to kiss you," he whispered in my ear.

"Eww!" I said like the idea of him kissing me all sweaty was super gross.

Matt laughed. "Later," he said. He had a look on his face like he couldn't wait for later to get here, and neither could I. I could hardly eat dinner. When we finally kissed on my front porch, Matt pulled me right into his lap and the way we kissed was . . . passionate. That word sounds weird, but it's the only word that fits. It was like a kiss in a movie that I'd never get sick of watching.

Thursday, May 15, 8:02 p.m.

Ugh. It can't be normal to be this indecisive. I wanted a second opinion, so I called Sophie. "What do you think I should do?" I asked when I'd finished explaining my dilemma.

"That's a tough one," said Sophie.

"I know." I nodded into the phone. I was glad she at least understood what I was going through.

"I don't know what to tell you because I've never gone to camp," she said. "I always go on vacation with my parents."

Maybe so, but I wanted Sophie to give me an opinion. "If you had to choose, what would you do?" I asked.

Sophie was quiet for a long time. "I'm just not sure," she said.

"OK. Thanks," I said to Sophie, like she'd been helpful. But she hadn't been. And to be honest, I don't really need her input. I think this is a decision only I can make.

Friday, May 16, 4:45 p.m.
On a bus
On the way to States

I still haven't decided what to do about camp. Mom and Dad asked me about it at breakfast, and I told them I wasn't sure yet.

"Think about it while you're away," said Dad.

I know my brain needs to be focused on the competition tomorrow, not on what I'm doing this summer. But as I sat on the bus next to Emily, I couldn't help thinking about it. If I brought it up to Emily, she'd say I'm crazy and ask why I want to go to camp when I have a super cute boyfriend at home.

No sense in asking her when I'm already asking myself that same question.

Saturday, May 17, 9:02 p.m.
Home from States
I decided

It's really weird how I decided. Something Ms. Baumann said helped me.

When we got to the hotel, she called a team

meeting. "The Faraway dance team has won twelve state titles," she said. "And I want to make it thirteen. This will take all of your dedication and focus tomorrow. You've all worked so hard. This is part of who you are. Now let's go finish what we started!"

Everyone clapped and cheered. And when they did, I remembered how much I love being part of this team. Like Ms. Baumann said, it's part of who I am, just like going to camp. I've always loved going to Camp Silver Shores. That thought stayed in my head all night last night and today, as we danced.

When the judges announced the winners, and we found out we'd WON, everyone on the team went crazy hugging and crying. It was one of the best moments of my life. I loved it, and I realized that even though camp is totally different from dancing, I love it just as much. And in that moment, I made my decision.

I'm going to camp.

Once I'd decided I felt so relieved, which has to mean I made the right decision.

Right?

When I told my family I'm going to camp, you would have thought I was some kind of hero. Mom put extra chocolate chips in my pancakes. Dad told me he's proud of "the maturity I'm showing." And May tried to give me her Mickey Mouse ears. It was all so nice, and it made me hopeful that Matt's reaction will be good too.

I'd be lying if I didn't say that I'm worried. Especially after how he reacted when I told him we won States. He almost didn't react. When I texted him from the bus ride home that we'd won, all he texted back was congrats, and it took him over an hour to write back.

I showed Emily his text (not that there was much to show). "He was probably doing something and that's why he didn't text back. Or maybe he's jealous. Didn't you say his baseball team came in second?" She waved it off like either way it was no big deal.

But it was kind of a big deal to me. I wasn't sure why he wasn't happier for me, especially after he'd been so sweet and supportive when

I told him I was scared about not doing well at Regionals.

I'm also not sure how he'll react when I tell him about camp. I tried to visualize his response.

Cool. No big deal. Camp sounds like fun. It's just four weeks, and when you get back, we'll hang out and watch movies and stuff.

There. That won't be so hard.

Monday, May 19, 6:05 p.m.
In my room

As soon as Dad got home from the diner today, he told me, "April, I sent in your registration and deposit for camp. It's official!"

"It's official!" screamed May.

"It's official?" I asked.

Dad nodded, confirming that everything was set. Maybe it was from his end, but I still had something I needed to take care of.

6:22 p.m.

I'm going to text Matt to see if he wants to walk his dog with me.

Unfortunately, he does. Oh God. Here goes.

Home from dog walking

This dog walk wasn't like my last one with Matt. It started fine. Matt was talking about how he's playing on a travel team this summer. "My team is playing in Birmingham, Mobile, and Atlanta." He paused and looked down at me like he was apologizing. "So I'll be gone a lot."

It was the perfect opportunity to tell him. I took a deep breath.

"I'll be gone some too," I said. Then I told him about Camp Silver Shores and how, except for last summer, I'd gone every summer since I was nine. "I love going to camp there," I added.

I looked at Matt like it was his turn to say something about camp or ask me why I love it, but he didn't. He just shrugged like he had no comment.

"I'll only be gone four weeks," I said, like it wasn't that much time. I looked at Matt again.

There was no trace of a smile on his face. "Are you mad I'm going?" I asked.

"Whatever," mumbled Matt. He barely looked at me after that.

I wasn't sure if I should say something else, but the truth is, I had no idea what I'd say. I'd felt so sure of my decision when I made it, but Matt's response was making me unsure all over again.

5:15 p.m.

I just called Sophie to tell her I'd decided to go to camp and how my conversation had gone with Matt, but before I could say anything, Sophie said she had some news for me.

"I'm coming to Faraway!" Then she told me her parents are going to Europe for the summer and that she's going to come and stay here, at Gaga and Willy's house, for six weeks.

I couldn't believe what I was hearing. "Why do you want to be in Faraway for the summer?"

Sophie laughed like it was a dumb question. "When you asked me about camp, it made me realize I've never done anything in the summer but travel around Europe with my parents. I want to have a real American teenage summer. What better place to do it than Faraway?"

I could think of a bunch of places, but apparently Sophie couldn't.

"When I told my parents that I want to come here, I thought for sure they would say no, but they agreed to it. Pretty quickly, actually. So now I have an opinion on what you should do this summer," said Sophie. "Stay home! I'll be there too."

I hated telling Sophie just as much as I hated telling Matt I'd decided to go to camp.

But she was cool. "We'll still have a week before you leave and a week when you get back to spend together," she said.

"That'll be great," I told her. And it will be. For me. But I can't imagine what Sophie is going to do for four weeks in Faraway.

Friday, May 23, 3:15 p.m.
Last day of school

The school year ended.

All the kids in Faraway are out and happy

and free and thinking about things like pools and beaches and bathing suits. I'm thinking about those things too, but I'm also thinking about the choice I made.

Dear God, please let it be a good one.

Oh please don't go—we'll eat

you up—we love you so!

—*The wild things*, Where the Wild Things Are

Monday, May 26
Memorial Day

Today Matt asked me if I wanted to go to the beach. He told me a bunch of kids were going and he wanted me to come too. But when I asked Mom and Dad, they said NO! And the reason they wouldn't let me go was so stupid. They didn't want me hanging out with a bunch of high school kids!

"I'm going to be one of those kids in three months!" I told them.

I shouldn't have had to remind Mom and Dad that I'm starting high school in August.

But no matter what I said, they wouldn't let me go, which was too bad because this is the first thing Matt has asked me to do since I told him I'm going to camp a week ago.

Wednesday, May 28, 4:45 p.m.
In my room

What I did today: helped May get ready for camp. It was fun. I helped her pick out what she should take and Mom ironed her name labels in as we picked.

What I didn't do (today or yesterday or unfortunately, the day before): see Matt.

After I told him I was going to camp, things were kind of weird between us. Then they got normal again. Then Monday, he asked me to go to the beach and I told him my mom and dad wouldn't let me go. What if he thought that was just an excuse and that I didn't want to go? What if he thinks I'm going to camp because I don't care about being with him?

I need to make sure he doesn't think that.

10:28 p.m.
Can't believe what I just did!

I just texted Matt to see if he wants to come over, and he said yes!

I would never say, *"Do you want to come to my front porch?"* He always just shows up, but I did it because I wanted to make sure he didn't think I didn't want to go to the beach on Monday.

He probably thinks I texted him because I want to make out. It's not that I don't want to make out, but I really want to tell him why I didn't go to the beach.

11:11 p.m.

Matt just left. We talked *and* we made out. We started kissing as soon as he got to my porch, but after a while, I pulled away and asked if he was mad I didn't go to the beach.

"Nah," he said. But he seemed kind of mad. "Are you mad I'm going to camp?"

"Nah," he said, then he pulled me back into him and we started kissing again.

I wasn't sure if "nah" meant he wasn't mad or if he just wanted to kiss and not talk. But when he left he said, "See you soon," which hopefully means he meant what he said when he said, "nah."

Monday, June 2, 4:30 p.m.
My talk with Sophie

I just spent the last forty-three minutes on the phone. We talked about a lot of things, but mainly we talked about Matt and why I didn't see him all weekend. I don't want to be the kind of girlfriend who dissects every little thing her boyfriend says, but the last time I saw him was last Wednesday night when I asked him to come to my front porch. When he left and said, "See you soon," it made me think I would, but I haven't.

I texted with him on Thursday and Friday, but I was the one who texted first. He didn't text or call all day Saturday, so Sunday, I texted him.

Me: What's up?
Matt: Nothin.
Me: Where've you been?
Matt: Around.

Me: Seems like I'm always the one who texts first.

(No response for 12 minutes.)

Me: ??

Matt (after 4 more minutes): Why does it matter who texts first?

Matt: ??

Me: (Not sure how to answer.)

Matt: I don't really like texting.

I wasn't sure if Matt meant in general or with me. When I talked to Sophie, I asked her if she thought he was saying he doesn't like texting with me.

"Probably not," she said. Then she added that guys are weird sometimes and that we could talk about that (and lots of other things) when she gets to Faraway on Friday.

Friday can't get here fast enough!

Friday, June 6, 10:45 p.m.
Sophie arrived!

I went with my dad to the airport in Mobile to pick up Sophie. "I can't believe you're here!"

I screamed when I saw her.

"I know! Me too!" Sophie was just as excited as I was, which honestly made me feel good because I truly don't think coming to Faraway is all that exciting. But I'm glad she does.

My whole family had dinner at Gaga and Willy's, and Sophie and I planned everything we're going to do for the next week before I leave for camp. We're going to have so much fun!

It's what I was thinking about as I was going to sleep tonight and heard the knock on my window. I hopped out of bed. This was the third night in a row (not that I'm counting) that Matt had come over. He's like a magician. Sometimes he's nowhere to be found, and then he mysteriously appears.

Whatever. I was excited to tell him about Sophie. "I can't wait for you to meet her!" I said. "It's so cool that she's here."

"Yeah," Matt said, but I could tell by the look on his face that he was kind of indifferent. He might not care that Sophie's in Faraway, but I'm glad she's here.

Monday, June 9, 8:45 p.m.

Sophie and I had such a fun weekend! We spent the weekend at Gaga's curled up in our PJs, watching romantic comedies, looking at old photo albums and baking cookies.

"Did you bring any real clothes?" Sophie's grandpa teased her. She did, but neither of us put them on. Sophie wanted Gaga to teach us how to knit even though I didn't want to learn.

"Try it," said Sophie. "Knitting is very retro."

Gaga gave me a told-you-so wink. But I didn't want to do it, so Gaga told Sophie she would teach her while I'm gone.

This morning, we finally got dressed and went on a bike ride with Billy and Brynn. It was the same ride Billy, Brynn, and I have always gone on—to Rock Creek, then on to Mr. Agee's farm to count cows, and then to 7-Eleven for Slurpees. "This is the closest I've ever been to a real cow," Sophie said as we settled in on Mr. Agee's fence.

"I guess they don't have many cows in New York City," said Billy.

Sophie laughed and told him they don't have any.

I could tell Billy thought that was funny. He was making jokes about the cows and he was being super friendly to Sophie. He asked her lots of questions about where she lived and her school and her friends. Brynn wasn't as friendly. She was actually kind of standoffish.

"I think she was upset that we're spending so much time together while you're here," I told Sophie when we got back to Gaga's. But Sophie disagreed.

"I think she didn't like that Billy was talking to me. I think she likes him. I mean, *likes* him." That's not news to Sophie. We've talked about it lots of times before.

But I reminded Sophie about the pact Brynn and Billy and I made this spring, that no one would be anything more than friends.

"I don't know," she said. "It seems like that's a pact Brynn might not want to keep."

"But Billy wouldn't break it," I said.

Sophie did a half-shrug, like it's hard to know.

Billy is a lot of things, but I just don't think of him as a pact breaker.

Wednesday, June 11, 4:45 p.m.
Sophie met Matt

Ever since Sophie arrived, she's been asking when she would meet Matt.

It wasn't like I wasn't trying. But every time I asked if he wanted to hang out, he was busy. Tonight was finally the night. Sophie and I were walking Gilligan, and we saw Matt coming home from a game. "He's even cuter in person!" Sophie whispered as he walked toward us in his uniform.

I gave Matt a come-over-and-meet-Sophie wave.

He walked towards us, but slowly, like he wasn't in a hurry to meet Sophie. And he wasn't very friendly. She was asking him all about baseball and his team, but he didn't ask her anything about herself.

Which seemed kind of weird. Like he didn't like her or something.

"What did you think of Matt?" I asked when we walked off.

Sophie turned and looked at him like she needed a second look before she could give her opinion. When she turned to look, my eyes followed hers, and I saw that Matt had turned to look back over his shoulder too. It was totally embarrassing. We were all looking at each other. Everyone turned around quickly, like no one wanted anyone else to know they'd been looking.

"So what'd you think?" I asked again.

"I'm not sure," said Sophie. She opened her mouth like she was going to add something, but she closed it again. I thought it was odd, because Sophie always says what's on her mind.

When I got home, I texted Matt and asked what he thought of Sophie. But he didn't respond. I don't know why, but his lack of an answer bothered me even more.

Friday, June 13, 10:42 p.m.
Good-byes

The first good-bye wasn't so bad.

We had a family going-away dinner for May and me at Gaga's. Everyone was there, including Sophie. Gaga had fondue pots set up, so we made beef and chicken fondue for dinner and then we had chocolate fondue for dessert. I don't know what gave her the idea, but everyone had fun doing it. When it was time to go home, I said bye to all my cousins and saved Sophie for last.

"I'm going to miss you!" I said as I gave her a hug.

"How do you think I feel?" said Sophie. "What am I going to do here for four weeks without you?"

"You'll have plenty of time to work on knitting your scarf and mittens."

Sophie laughed. "Maybe I'll make a blanket too."

"Good idea," I told her. Then I leaned closer. "Keep an eye on Matt while I'm gone," I whispered.

"Will do," said Sophie.

Then we hugged one last time and I left. Saying bye to her wasn't easy. We'd had so much fun together since she arrived, and part of me didn't want to go. Plus, I knew I'd have to say good-bye to Matt next. I don't want to sound like a drama queen, but I was kind of picturing Matt and me kissing and saying it would be hard to be apart for four weeks. But the real good-bye was nothing like that.

When I got home from Gaga's, I kept checking my phone to see if he'd called or texted. But he hadn't. He knew I had to get up early to go on the camp bus, so it kind of sucked that he hadn't tried to make a plan to say bye. By nine I still I hadn't heard from him, so I texted him. I told him he should come over sooner vs. later because my parents would think it was weird if we didn't say good-bye.

He came over, but it seemed like he only did because he felt like he had to.

When he walked into the den, I tried to give my family a look like they should excuse themselves, but they didn't. They just stuck around, so all Matt ended up saying was pretty lame stuff like bye and have fun.

When he was leaving, I walked him out the door. We were standing on my front porch. Our place. I finally had a minute alone with him.

"I won't have my phone at camp," I told him.

"So you won't be able to text me."

Matt shrugged like that wasn't a problem.

"But you can write," I said. "I'll write to you too."

Matt raised his eyebrows like someone just asked him to shave his head. "I'm not much of a letter writer," he said.

"I'll miss you," I said. And this time I wasn't even embarrassed to say it.

But Matt just looked at me like he wasn't sure what he was going to say. Then he leaned over and gave me a quick kiss on the lips. "Yeah, me too," he said, and he left.

But I wasn't convinced. I'm also not convinced that going to camp is a good idea.

I repeated the prayer I made the last day of school. But this time, I squeezed my eyes shut and prayed like I really meant it.

Dear God, please, please let this be a good choice.

If you never did, you should. These

things are fun and fun is good.

—Dr. Seuss

Saturday, June 14, 4:45 p.m.

Day 1

Camp is off to a great start. I was a little worried about how May would do, given that just last year, her main approach to socializing was to show off her strength by picking people up. But she was the first one off the bus, and by the time I found her to make sure she'd met her counselor, she was already chatting with the girls in her bunk like they'd known each other forever.

It's really cool to be on the senior side, too. My bunk is huge. My closest camp friends, Talia, Meg, Karina, and of course, Brynn, are all in it, and we have the coolest counselors, Ellen (who was a Silver Lake camper and the counselor Brynn and I both wanted) and Sandy (a new counselor from Texas who is a cheerleader at her college and seems really fun.) But the best part about being back is that right when I got off the bus, my friends were waiting for me.

"She's back!" screamed Karina as they all grabbed and hugged me.

It felt like I hadn't missed a day. I think I made the right decision to come.

Sunday, June 22, 1:30 p.m.
Rest hour
Week 1 wrap-up

I kind of feel like I should do a week in review. But I don't have time or really want to. It has been an amazing first week of camp. (I know that's a pathetic summary. Camp is busy!) I definitely made the right decision to come. I'm having so much fun that I haven't really thought about what's going on at home.

I haven't heard from Sophie (or Matt) telling me what's going on.

I'll be completely honest here. I'd like a letter.

Tuesday, June 24, 1:17 p.m.
Mail arrived

I never thought that getting a letter could be worse than not getting one, but it is.

I got a letter today from Sophie, and all she wrote about was hanging out with Gaga and knitting. Seriously? Why she would want to do that, I don't know. But that's not what bothered me. What I thought was weird is that she didn't answer any of the questions I asked her in my letter, like: Have you seen Matt? What's he been doing? Does it seem like he misses me?

She didn't even mention Matt. The only explanation that makes any sense is that she didn't answer any of those questions because she wrote her letter to me before she got mine.

I'm not going to let this bother me.

But I'll feel better when I get her next letter and hear what's going on.

Friday, June 27, 10:02 p.m.
After campfire

Something weird happened tonight after campfire. Brynn and Billy and I always hang out together, but tonight, I couldn't find either one of them. It's like they both disappeared. I asked around, and no one had seen them.

When I got back to my bunk, Brynn was there. "Where'd you go after campfire?" I asked. "I was looking everywhere for you."

"I went with Ellen to pick up the cabin snacks," she answered.

But it was weird for two reasons. One, she knows the three of us always hang out after campfire. And two, when she said she went to pick up the snacks, I saw her glance at the table with the milk and cookies on it like she wanted to make sure they were there.

What I'm about to say sounds bad, I know. I have no reason to think she was lying, but something in me didn't believe she'd gone to get the snacks.

Saturday, June 28, 8:45 a.m.
After breakfast

I decided to ask Billy where he was after campfire last night.

"I don't remember," said Billy when I asked him.

I made a face like it was a ridiculous answer, which we both knew it was because Billy doesn't forget anything. Billy shrugged like it wasn't a big deal and I shouldn't be making it into one. So I let it go. But it bothered me.

Sunday, June 29
A weird thing happened in sailing
Actually it happened after sailing

Today after we'd brought the boats in, Cecily, the head sailing counselor, asked Billy and me if we could help her clean them out. It doesn't sound like that would be fun, but it was. Cecily gave us rags and scrub brushes and squirt soap and buckets and we got really into what Billy called "giving the boats a bath."

We were cleaning and I was laughing as Billy made dirty boat jokes. When I least expected it, Billy threw a huge bucket of soapy water on me. I had to get him back, which meant we both ended up soaking wet and laughing.

It was great, but it made me realize that it was the first thing Billy and I have done alone together since we got to camp. I mentioned it to Brynn when I got back to the cabin. I told her how much fun it was hanging out with him. "I know we broke up and everything, but I wonder why we're not as close at camp as we used to be."

"Hmmm," said Brynn, like that was an answer to my question.

But it wasn't.

Tuesday, July 1, 1:14 p.m.
More mail

I haven't gotten a letter from Matt yet. He told me he's not a letter writer, so I kind of didn't expect to. But I did get another letter from Sophie, and there was no mention of Matt in it! Not a word. I looked on the front of her letter, the back, I even double checked inside the envelope to see if she'd put a special note or something in it. But there was nothing. It's really weird, too, because I've written her at least four letters asking if she's seen him and what he's up to. I wish I could call her and find out what's going on. Campers are only allowed to make emergency phone calls. I know the secretary in the office would say this isn't one.

But I'm beginning to think it is.

Wednesday, July 2, 5:18 p.m.
Bunk beauty day

I canNOT believe what I saw today. It's almost too embarrassing to write about.

We had beauty day in my bunk. Everyone showered, shaved, deep conditioned their hair, and put on seaweed masks. We were all sitting around with our towels wrapped around us and talking while we were waiting for our masks to dry. When Brynn's mask was dry, she took off her towel to get back in the shower, and when she did I saw her boobs.

That makes it sound like I was looking. But I wasn't.

I couldn't help what I saw. Even though

we're in the same bunk, it's the first time I've seen them with nothing on them, and I couldn't believe how big they were. I can't be the only who has noticed. I'm sure every boy in camp has too.

And mainly, the boy I'm thinking about is Billy.

If I had a flower for every time
I thought of you . . . I could walk
through my garden forever.

—*Claudia Adrienne Grandi*

~~Happy~~ July 4!
Not so happy, actually

The Fourth of July is supposed to be the best day of camp, and for lots of people it was. But today was literally the worst day of my life. I know I've said that before. I don't want to be the girl who cried wolf, but this time I truly mean it.

It started this morning in my bunk when we were getting ready for the all-day celebration at the waterfront. Everyone was putting on bathing suits and flip-flops.

"OMG!" screamed Karina. "Look at that!"

When she screamed, everyone looked to see what she was talking about, and it was Brynn. She had on a red, white, and blue bikini that I didn't even know she had.

"That's. The. Cutest. Suit. Ever." Talia enunciated each word, which somehow made her statement indisputable.

"You look so good," said Meg.

Then everyone started talking about what an amazing body Brynn has. I could tell she loved the way she looked too. She didn't even put on a cover-up. "What's the point," she said to no one in particular as she walked out of the bunk. "I'm going to take it off as soon as I get to the beach."

Her good mood continued when we arrived. A lot of the boys noticed her right when we got to the waterfront, and Billy was one of them. "Look at you!" he said to Brynn as he walked towards us. He was grinning like he liked what he saw.

Brynn was beaming. Their interchange put me in a non-celebratory mood, which only worsened as the whole camp was divided into three teams. Billy and Brynn were both on the red team. As we spent the morning competing in relays and contests, I couldn't help looking in their direction. Every time I did, they were right next to each other and smiling.

It kind of depressed me to see it.

At lunch, May actually came over to my table and asked if I was OK. "The tacos gave me a stomachache," she said, like that had to be my problem too.

I wish bad meat was what had me so upset.

All afternoon Billy and Brynn stayed side by side while the teams competed in a sing-off, a cheer-a-thon and tug-of-war. When Director Dan, who has been running the camp for as long as we've all been going there, announced that the red team won, my eyes immediately went to Billy and Brynn. The kids on their team went crazy over their victory, and I saw Billy give Brynn a swooping hug. Her feet came off the ground, and his arms were wrapped tightly around her back. As I watched his hands linger on her back even after he'd put her down, a sense of dread bubbled up inside me.

We came back to the bunk after the nighttime festivities and fireworks, but Brynn was nowhere in sight. When she finally came back to the bunk, I tried not to watch as she huddled with Talia and Karina and talked quietly to both of them. She had the happiest look on her face that I've ever seen. Talia and Karina both hugged her. When they finished hugging, Brynn and I made eye contact. She knew I was watching, and she looked away.

It made me feel sick. Literally. The happy look on Brynn's face plus the fact that she told other people (and not me) what was clearly making her so happy, plus the fact that when she saw me looking at her she looked away, can only add up to one thing.

My best friends are a couple.

Even though no one has told me, I know. And I don't like the way it feels. I guess Brynn used to feel the same way when Billy and I were going out. But this is different. Billy used to be my boyfriend. So it's even weirder. He's with her now.

Part of me can't help but wonder if she's been planning and plotting so that this would happen. That sounds terrible of me to say, but it just makes everything seem so cloudy.

I think back to the day in her room when I confided in her about not seeing or hearing from Matt and how much it upset me. It was like her attitude about him shifted overnight. One minute she couldn't stand him, and the next she totally accepted him. At the time, I thought she was being a good friend and trying to make me feel better. But now I'm wondering if it was part of some grand master plan to make sure I stayed with Matt so she could have Billy all to herself.

I don't know. It honestly makes me doubt all the nice things she's done for me lately. Did she try to plan a party for me and give me an extra-nice gift because she knew this would happen and she didn't want me to be mad if it did?

My head hurts. I just can't believe Billy and Brynn are a couple. The more I think about them as a couple, the more I think about Matt.

At least I have a boyfriend at home. At least I hope I do. I haven't heard from him. Or about him. I want to go home. I really do. I never should have come. And when I do go home, I want things to be just as I left them.

Dear God, Please.

All that we see or seem is but a dream

within a dream.

—*Edgar Allen Poe*

Saturday, July 5, 11:39 a.m.
Before lunch

It's confirmed. I found out in waterskiing that Brynn and Billy are a couple.

"Can you believe Brynn and Billy are going out?" Stacey Abbot said.

"I think it's cute it happened on the fourth of July," said Amanda Pascale, another girl in my bunk. They both looked at me like they wanted to see what I thought.

"Brynn and Billy are going out?" I asked.

Stacey and Amanda looked at each other like they'd just said something they shouldn't have. I could tell they assumed I knew. Why wouldn't they? Brynn and I are supposed to be best friends. You would think she'd tell me something like that.

But she didn't. I guess she didn't want to tell me she's going out with my ex. Everyone knows that's something you're NOT supposed to do. But here's something else you're not supposed to do: tell everyone BUT your best friend when you start going out with somebody. How could Brynn not tell me?

Did she think I wasn't going to find out? Hmmm.

2:15 p.m.
Talked to Brynn

It wasn't like I initiated it. I mean, what was I supposed to say? *Hey, why didn't you tell me you're dating my ex?* But I think Brynn could tell I was pissed because she came over to me at rest hour. "You've been giving me dirty looks ever since waterskiing. What's your problem?" she asked, like I was the one who had done something wrong.

I couldn't believe how defensive she was acting. I didn't bother beating around the bush. "Are you and Billy going out?"

"You know, you're not always the easiest person to talk to," she said, like that was an answer to my question.

Before I could say anything else, she went off on me. "You act like Billy is still yours, and he's not," she said.

I could feel myself starting to get mad. "What are you talking about?"

"Like the day when you were helping him clean out the sailboats."

I had to think for a second, but then it dawned on me what she meant. When I told Brynn how much fun I'd had hanging out with Billy, it made her jealous. But I hadn't done anything wrong. "Cecily asked Billy and me to help her," I said.

Brynn ignored my answer. "You should be happy for me," she said. "You already have a boyfriend. Now I have one too."

I knew that was Brynn's way of saying this conversation was over.

5:40 p.m.

I still can't believe Brynn didn't tell me. But neither did Billy.

6:55 p.m.
Talked to Billy

After dinner, I confronted Billy. I told him I knew about Brynn and him.

"Yep. I was going to tell you," he said, like talking to me was on his to-do list and he just hadn't gotten to it yet. But Billy seemed uncomfortable.

Or maybe I was just projecting my own discomfort onto him.

Pact breakers. Both of them.

Tuesday, July 8, 10:02 p.m.

It has been four days since Billy and Brynn started going out. Three since I've known about it, and I still can't get over it. My best friends are a couple. Billy is my ex-boyfriend. Everyone in my bunk knows the situation, and they've all asked me if I'm cool with it.

"Of course!" I keep saying like I am. But it's like a tetanus shot. It just hurts for longer than you'd like it to.

Wednesday, July 9, 1:15 p.m.
Post mail pickup

Today makes it officially five days that Billy and Brynn have been going out. It has been really weird. It's not like I ever talk to them about it. It's almost like they both try to avoid me, like I make them uncomfortable.

This morning I was in the craft shop with my bunk and we were tie-dyeing T-shirts. Brynn was at a table with Talia and Karina, and they were all working on their shirts and laughing so I decided to join them.

"I love the shirt you're making," I said to Brynn. I wanted to at least try to make things seem normal.

"Thanks!" she said a little too sweetly. Then she said, "I guess I'm done."

I don't know if she was or wasn't, but she

took her shirt and went and hung it up on the clothesline. Instead of coming back to the table where Karina and Talia and I were working, she walked into the supply closet like she was looking for something.

Would Brynn rather spend time in a supply closet than with me?

Apparently, yes.

Thursday, July 10
Time doesn't matter

I got another letter from Sophie. She went on and on and on about the scarf and gloves she's knitting, the PBS miniseries she's been watching with her grandpa, how she's trying to teach Gaga to work the DVR, the brownies she baked for my younger cousins, and that she helped Amanda tone down on her makeup and how much Amanda likes it. But she didn't mention one word about Matt in response to my last letter to her, which said:

Dear Sophie,
How are you? How's Matt? Have you seen

him? Did he say anything about me? I'm kind of freaking out. Please write me a letter and ONLY talk about Matt.

Thanks!

Love, April

In fact, Sophie wrote me a letter and talked about everything BUT Matt. Two words: too weird.

I just want to go home.

Still Thursday, July 10
Nostalgic

Dad always says life is about perspective, and I guess that's true. May came up to me before dinner and said, "I'm so sad we have to go home on Saturday."

I brushed her stick-straight bangs out of her eyes. "I know," I said. "It's hard to leave." Even though I didn't think it was going to be so hard this year, I could feel her pain. For so many years, I felt exactly the same way. Everything seemed so simple when I was younger.

I wish it still was.

Friday, July 11
Last day of camp.

I'm going home tomorrow. I'll feel much better when I know it's just as I left it.

All good things must come to an end.

Ancient proverb

Saturday, July 12 1:45 p.m.
In my own room

It's good to be home.

Mom, Dad, and June picked May and me up from the bus. Even though I was quiet, I enjoyed listening to May tell them how awesome camp was. And Dad made my favorite lunch. After eating camp food for a month, it was great coming home to a hot plate of homemade fried chicken and mashed potatoes.

I kept waiting for Mom and Dad to ask me about camp. They did, but in a vague kind of non-meddling way. It was almost as if they intuitively got that something must have happened that I didn't want to talk about. It was a good start. As soon as I shower and get rid of the camp grunge look, I'm going to see Matt! I hope that's good too.

2:59 p.m.
Home from Matt's
Not so good

I didn't stay long. Twenty-three minutes to be exact. But I could have just stayed for three and I think Matt would have been happier.

He answered the door when I rang the bell. He looked cuter than ever. He was super tan and shirtless. He hadn't cut his hair all summer, and it was blonder than ever, I guess from spending so much time outside at the baseball field. I gave him a cute, happy-to-see-you smile, but he didn't smile back. "I just got back from camp," I said.

He ran a hand through his hair. "How was it?" he asked after a long hesitation.

"Fun," I said.

Matt shifted from one foot to the other. But he didn't say anything back like, "Fun, how?" or "Tell me about it."

He just stood there, doing the Matt Parker quiet thing, so I rambled on a little bit about camp. But he didn't seem interested. "How's your team doing?" I asked.

"Fine," said Matt. He looked down at his hand and scratched a spot on his thumb.

"Do you have a bug bite?" I asked. I regretted the question as soon as it left my mouth. Matt looked down at his hand and stopped scratching. "No," he said. Then he just looked at me. I wasn't sure what to do.

"I just wanted to say hi and tell you I'm back!" I tried to say the words in a light, happy, no-big-deal way.

"OK." Matt did his head-bob thing, and then he closed the door as I turned to leave. No hug. No kiss. Barely a smile. He seemed super distracted. Maybe something happened with baseball, or his dad, or he just wasn't in the mood to talk. I probably just caught him at a bad time.

As Ms. Baumann says, timing is everything.

I can't believe what just happened. In my wildest dreams I never would have expected it.

After I left Matt's, I went to see Sophie. I texted her as I was walking to Gaga's that I would be there in less than 90 seconds. That's how excited I was to see her.

But I could tell something was off with Sophie as soon as she opened the door. She seemed anxious, which is a very un-Sophie-like thing to be. She gave me a hug, but it was awkward. As we started to talk, she barely made eye contact with me. "Is everything OK?" I asked as we walked toward the Cold Shack.

"Yeah," said Sophie. But I wasn't convinced.

"So how was it being in Faraway for the summer?" I couldn't wait to ask her what I really wanted to know.

Sophie talked about how she knitted during the day with Gaga and watched TV with her grandpa at night.

I made a face. "Sounds boring," I said.

Sophie laughed. She seemed to be feeling

more comfortable. "It was fun."

I couldn't wait any longer. "Did you see Matt?" I had to ask.

All traces of Sophie's smile disappeared. We were already in line. "Let's get our ice cream," said Sophie. "Then we'll talk."

She made it sound like we had something to talk about. As we settled into a booth, I instinctively knew I wasn't going to like hearing what Sophie had to say.

As soon as we sat down, she confirmed it.

"April, something happened this summer and I just need to be totally honest with you. I couldn't sit at Gaga's all day and knit. One day Amanda called and asked if I wanted to go to the pool. It sounded like fun, so I went."

She paused. "I saw Matt at the pool." She paused again. "It wasn't a big deal. He just asked how I was doing and if I was having fun in Faraway."

I wanted to ask if he asked about me but I didn't. The answer seemed obvious. My stomach was in knots.

Sophie continued. "I told him that I pretty

much was just hanging out with Gaga and my grandpa all day. It was the truth. Matt said I should come to one of his baseball games. He said that lots of kids go and it would be a good way to meet people."

I felt ice cream dripping down my hand. I hadn't taken a bite of my cone.

Sophie kept talking. "So I went to a game. It seemed like it would be fun. Kind of an all-American thing to do that I'd never done."

I watched as Sophie took a deep breath and swallowed. I knew the worst part of the story was still coming.

Sophie continued, but her words seemed slower and more measured, like she was thinking about each one before she said it. "As I was leaving the game, Matt caught up with me. I was walking back towards Gaga's house, and he sort of fell into place beside me. We were going the same direction, so it wasn't like I could tell him not to walk with me."

Sophie looked at me to see how I was handling what she was saying. I tried to appear calm, but I wasn't feeling it.

"We walked home through a park, and he told me it was called Central Park. I told him that was cool because we have a Central Park in New York. When I said that, he told me this park has much cooler places. I said no way, and he said he'd show me one."

I felt the chicken and mashed potatoes I'd had for lunch turn over in my stomach.

As Sophie continued with her story, her voice picked up speed. "Matt took me inside this little circle of trees. I told him it was cool because it was like a little room no one could see in."

Sophie paused but only for a second. "When I said that, Matt tried to kiss me. As soon as he did, I pulled away. I got really mad. I told him that I couldn't believe he'd done that."

I started to get up. I had to get out of there. I thought I was going to be sick. But Sophie grabbed my hand and wouldn't let me leave.

"April, that's all that happened. I swear. I haven't even seen Matt since then. It didn't mean anything. I don't know why Matt did it. Maybe he thought I was flirting with him when I told him no one could see us. But I didn't mean it like that. Or maybe he just missed you and he was with me but thinking about you. I don't know why it happened. I've thought about it a thousand different ways, and I honestly just think it was Matt being a dumb guy. I would have told you about it in a letter, but I didn't want to upset you at camp."

I couldn't speak. Tears were rolling down my cheeks. Neither Sophie nor I had touched our ice cream. Sophie squeezed my hand. "April, I'm so sorry, but I couldn't *not* tell you now that you're back."

"Yeah," I said like I was glad she had.

But I wasn't sure if I was. I wasn't sure about anything.

10:02 p.m.
In my room
Alone

I have been here for hours. My eyes are puffy and swollen. My family keeps trying to come in my room. Sophie has called and texted a bunch of times. She feels terrible. I told her I appreciate her honesty and that I'm not mad at her. I just don't want to talk. To her or to anyone.

I still can't believe it.

I shouldn't have gone to camp. If I'd stayed home, none of this would have happened. I wish my parents had made me go. Then I could at least blame someone.

But I've got no one to blame but myself.

No, scratch that. There's one more person to blame.

Matt Parker.

If you're going through hell,

keep going.

—*Winston Churchill*

Sunday, July 13, 9:02 a.m.
Should still be asleep

How can I sleep when Sophie keeps calling me? "You have to talk to Matt," she said for the third time this morning.

I wished she would just let this go. "I told you. I don't know what to say to him." I didn't know how to make it any clearer.

"It's simple," said Sophie, who was ignoring what I'd said.

"You think everything is simple." My tone was too sharp. I wanted to be mad at Sophie even though I knew what happened wasn't her fault.

She could tell. "April, I'm sorry. I didn't mean talking to Matt would be easy. I meant when you talk to him, you simply need to ask him why he did it and how he feels about you."

"So you want me to tell him you told me what happened?" I ask.

"I don't have anything to hide," said Sophie.

"OK. I'll do that," I said. But to be honest, I'm not sure what I'm going to do.

9:45 a.m.

While I was pretending to eat breakfast so Mom and Dad would stop asking what's wrong, I was trying to decide what to do.

Should I talk to Matt? Even though Sophie was so clear about how she'd handle it, I'm not sure how I want to handle it. I'd like another opinion. I could talk to Emily, but she'd tell me I shouldn't have gone to camp. I'd really like to talk to Brynn, but we're not really talking about anything. It's not that we're not talking. We're both just sort of pretending like we don't both know that I'm upset about the fact that she and Billy are a couple and it's something we've never really talked about.

That only leaves one other person.

11:59 a.m.
Back from Billy's

It was a little weird to talk to Billy about what happened with Matt. I mean, given our history, it was probably the last thing he wanted to talk about, but he gave me some good advice.

"You have to talk to him," said Billy. "You're supposed to be in a relationship. It's not OK that he just kissed someone else."

I tried to ignore the awkwardness between us. It was more than I could deal with, but we both knew that's what I did to Billy when we were going out.

"I'm sorry," said Billy. "I didn't mean to make you feel bad. You're one of my best friends. I just want you to be happy. Talk to Matt. You'll feel better."

"Thanks," I told Billy. He was right. He almost always is.

Then he looked at me and paused. "Hey,

I'm sorry about everything with Brynn." I don't think he meant he was sorry they were going out. Just that he was sorry that it was hard for me.

"It's OK," I said. Just having him acknowledge it made me feel better. It also made me realize how much I miss talking to him. Even though I don't feel the same way about him that I do about Matt, it's hard not to love Billy. He's just so Billy.

I'm just starting to wish Matt wasn't so . . . Matt.

3:15 p.m.
In my room
With Gilligan

I talked to Matt. I kept thinking about it all day and trying to decide how and when and what I was going to say. Finally, I decided to just go over there and say whatever came out.

As soon as Matt answered his door, I started talking. I knew if I didn't, I'd chicken out. "Sophie told me what happened." I waited for him to respond.

But he didn't confirm or deny anything. He just stood there, feeling his abs. Usually I like watching him do that. Today it made me feel sick.

I kept going. "I don't understand how you could do that. We seemed close before I left for camp. You told me you *really* liked me."

It was definitely Matt's turn to say something. But he was being so annoyingly Matt. How could he just stand there not saying anything? I'd come to find out how he was feeling, and I was determined to do so. "So do you like Sophie?" I asked. My voice was rising. My words were coming faster. "Or me? Do you still *really like* me?"

Matt blinked like my questions were too rapid-fire to answer.

The confidence I'd felt just seconds earlier drained out of me. "Do you still like me?" My voice was softer.

But I could tell by the look on Matt's face that I wasn't going to like his answer.

Matt took a breath. "I think we need to take a break."

I looked down. I was scared if I looked at Matt, I'd start crying. "Does that mean we're breaking up?"

"Let's see how things are when school starts," said Matt.

"Sure," I said, like that was fine.

But it wasn't. As I walked home, Matt's words replayed in my head. *Let's see how things are when school starts.* I fail to see how they'll be any different. Nothing is going to happen that will erase the fact that he tried to kiss Sophie or that when I asked him about it, he refused to tell me why he did it or how he feels about her. Or how he feels about me.

For that matter, how do I feel about him?

a) Mad.

b) Dumped.

c) Disillusioned.

I'm going with d) All of the above.

6:45 p.m.
Crying

Mom, Dad, May, and June know I'm upset. I haven't come out of my room all afternoon.

They just tried to get me to come eat dinner. I'm not hungry.

"You have to eat," Mom just said through the door.

Why?

8:02 p.m.
Brynn just left

Billy texted me to see if I'd talked to Matt and how I was doing. I told him terrible, and he must have told Brynn because she came over to see me.

I could tell she felt a little weird about it because I hadn't told her what happened, but she didn't let that stop her. "Billy told me you could use some girl love." She got in bed beside me and pulled the covers up over both of us. "What now?" she asked.

Even though I'd been upset before she came, and truthfully, even more upset when she walked into my room without warning, her words made me smile. It's what she used to say when she slept over when we were little. As soon as my mom would turn out the light, she always wanted to know what we were going to do next.

"We could play *When I Grow Up*," I said.

Now it was her turn to smile. Brynn always loved that game.

"OK," she said, clearing her throat. "When I grow up I want to be a journalist." I gave her a *duh* look. "I'm not finished," she said. "And I want every room in my house to be decorated in turquoise."

I shook my head. We'd gone down this route before. "A whole house in one color is tacky," I reminded her.

Brynn pursed her lips like that was perhaps a true statement, but one she'd forgotten. "You're right," she said. Then she looked me. "And when I grow up I want to have you as my best friend so you can remind me not to make my whole house all one color."

I teared up all over again. I knew this wasn't about color schemes.

"April, I'm sorry about Matt. I know how much you like him. But I really came to say that I'm sorry about everything with Billy." She rested her head on my shoulder, and we stayed like that for a long time.

"I really hope we'll always be best friends," she said.

"Yeah," I said, like I hoped so too, but we both knew being grown up was a lot more complicated than playing it.

10:54 p.m.

I just took off the necklace Matt gave me, which got me thinking about all the conversations we had. I know that sounds dramatic, but it's like my brain wanted to do a mental review of everything we ever talked about. Not just about the big things like our relationship, but about the little things too, like baseball. For some reason, Matt's explanation of batting averages stuck in my head. I remember exactly what he told me. A batting average is the number of hits a player has in comparison to the number of times he's at bat.

I looked in my jewelry box at the necklace Matt gave me next to the bracelet from Billy. I guess when your batting average is zero, at least there's nowhere to go but up.

There's an end to every storm.

—*Meredith Grey*

Friday, July 18, 4:45 p.m.
I know how to knit

For the last five days, Sophie has been like an activities director for girls who get dumped. "The only way to get over a boy is to stay busy," said Sophie. So that's what we've been doing all week. I call it Camp Sophie.

We did yoga every morning in Gaga's backyard, followed by a run. She taught me how to make a croque monsieur, which is the French version of a ham and cheese sandwich but much more delicious. She had Gaga demonstrate her

DVR skills, and she taught me how to knit. Sort of. Actually, it was Gaga's idea, but I know Sophie was in on it.

"We should teach April how to knit," said Gaga.

"April doesn't want to learn to knit," I said.

Sophie and Gaga gave each other conspiratorial winks, like it had already been decided.

So this week I learned to knit and purl, and I not only finished two ski caps, but also ended up crying (some) and talking (a lot) to Sophie and Gaga about what happened with Matt, and it was totally therapeutic. I knew Sophie would be a good listener, but Gaga surprised me. She really rose to the occasion.

Basically, she and Sophie came up with three theories about what happened with Matt.

Theory #1: He's a boy. That was Sophie's. She said that while factually unsubstantiated, in her opinion 90 percent of boys under the age of sixteen are hopelessly and impossibly immature, incapable of making consistently good decisions, and that Matt falls squarely into that category.

Theory #2: He's from California. That one

was Gaga's. She said she's never been there, but from everything she's read, they do things differently out West. Her talk of "free love" and noncommitment actually made me laugh. I think the last time she read anything about California must have been in the sixties, but I appreciated her efforts.

Theory #3: He has problems with intimacy, like, in the sense of getting and staying close with someone, and just not being a jerk. Sophie and Gaga agreed this had to be Matt's issue. They both said that based on how hot and cold he was when we were going out, that had to be why Matt wasn't the best boyfriend.

They might be on to something. What they didn't know, what no one in Faraway but me knows, is what happened with Matt's dad. I'm no psychologist, but what he and his mom got away from . . . it must still be hard on Matt. But even if that's the case, how could I not be mad at him? It wasn't something I could discuss with Sophie or Gaga.

Anyway, none of their theories really gave me the answers I was looking for. Still, just talking to them made me feel better.

"Thanks for everything this week," I said to both of them at the end of one of what we've affectionately termed my "boy therapy sessions."

"No biggie," said Gaga. I know she'd heard Brynn and me say that for years and was trying to show me she's capable of being cool.

"You know, I don't really say that anymore," I told Gaga.

She nodded like she got it and put her arm around me. "We all grow up. It isn't always easy," she said. "But we all do it."

It was kind of a sappy thing to say, but it made me feel better.

Lately, growing up has sucked. I felt like I was in love with Matt. I still feel that way. At least I think I do. Every time I thought about it this week, I would get emotional. Part of me is so mad. Another part wishes we could just go back to how we were when Matt said he really liked me. But whenever I'd start to think about it and tear up, Sophie and Gaga would look at me and say, "Keep knitting!"

Here's the good news: if Matt and I ever

do get back together, I've got a nice ski cap for him.

Sunday, July 20, 12:45 p.m.
Sophie's going-away brunch

This morning we had a family brunch at the diner for Sophie. She's flying back to New York this afternoon, and everyone wanted the chance to tell her good-bye. When it was time for her to go, everyone hugged her and told her how much they'd miss her.

"It was fun having you here," said June. She gave Sophie a big hug and thanked her for playing Barbies with her while May and I were at camp.

Amanda, who is typically not a hugger, gave her a hug too. "I'll miss your makeup tips," she told Sophie.

"We'll miss you," said Charlotte.

"And your brownies," said Izzy.

"Yeah," said Harry. I wasn't sure if that meant he'd miss her or her brownies, but it was one of the nicest things I'd ever heard Harry say.

I raised a was-there-anyone-you-didn't-hang-out-with-this-summer eyebrow at her. Sophie shrugged like she got it and laughed. It was infectious. Even though I was sad she was leaving, I was smiling too.

Sophie's grandpa gave her a big hug and said, "I'm not going to miss you one bit!" But he was misty-eyed when he said it, and everyone knew he was joking. She gave him a big squeeze as Gaga held out her arms for a hug.

"It was so nice having you here," Gaga said to Sophie. It was easy to see how much Gaga loved her visit.

"I'm going to miss being here." I could tell by the way Sophie said it that she meant it.

I waited until everyone was done before I said my good-bye. "I'm going to miss you so much!" I whispered in Sophie's ear as I hugged her.

She hugged me back. Hard. I felt myself getting emotional again. I looked at Sophie. There were tears in her eyes too. "C'mon," she said, like she didn't want to leave me like that.

"We have to get going," said Uncle Drew, who was driving Sophie to the airport in

Mobile. Sophie and I gave each other one last hug as she got into Uncle Drew's car. I stood outside the diner and waved to her until the car was no longer in sight.

Then I walked home with May and June while Mom stayed to help Dad clean up.

It was a quiet morning in Faraway, and I actually enjoyed the quiet walk home with my sisters. I guess they were enjoying the solitude too. It was the first time I'd felt peaceful in a long time.

It felt good.

Follow the yellow brick road.

—The Wizard of Oz

Friday, July 25
In my room
Can't believe what I just heard

One minute I was talking to May about starting middle school, and in the middle of our conversation, she burst into tears. "What if I start my period at school?" she wailed. I knew what she was thinking. I remember being terrified of blood running down my legs and everyone laughing.

"Don't worry. It's normal to think the worst will happen, but it almost never does." I looped a big-sisterly arm around her. "Brynn and I used to worry about the same thing."

I think that made her feel better. We had just gone back to talking about switching classes and cafeteria food when my phone rang. It was Sophie. "I have some bad news and some good news," she said. Then she added, "I guess it's all in how you look at things."

She sounded like Gaga. I'm sure she heard her say that this summer. I couldn't believe what she said next.

"My parents are separating. They told me when I got home from Faraway," said Sophie. She told me how she cried all week and that the only thing that's kind of good is that it's a "*trial*" separation. Sophie said the word like she'd heard it a lot. I wanted to ask her exactly what it meant, but I had the feeling I shouldn't.

"I'm so sorry," I said quietly into the phone.

"I just don't understand it," she said. "I thought my parents were head over heels for each other. I mean, everyone always says how amazing they look together."

I thought about the first time I met Sophie

and her parents at Gaga and Willy's wedding. I thought her mother was so beautiful and her dad was so handsome, and they had Sophie, a perfect-looking daughter. They were the most stylish, chic family I'd ever seen.

"I guess it wasn't enough," Sophie said and then paused. "Before I left, I thought things were a little tense. I was surprised they let me come to Faraway, but I didn't know they had real problems."

Then Sophie started filling me in on the details. How her parents took her out to dinner to her favorite restaurant when she got back from Faraway and how she thought the night was going to be a coming-home party so they could hear all about her summer. "For most of the dinner, they didn't even say anything. They just kept looking at each other funny, and when dessert came, they told me, and I've hardly stopped crying since."

I felt terrible hearing how upset she'd been. "You should have called me."

"Yeah." Sophie sounded like she appreciated what I was saying. "I guess I wasn't ready to talk about it. I thought I could talk some sense into my parents. You know, convince them to stay together or something. But I couldn't." She paused. "I kind of feel like it's my fault. Maybe if I hadn't come to Faraway, they'd still be together."

"Sophie, it's not your fault. Your parents probably had a lot to talk about this summer, you know? Maybe it was better that they didn't do it in front of you."

Sophie accepted that explanation without argument. "My dad is moving back to Paris."

"What about you and your mom?" I asked. I was thinking about how much Sophie loves New York and how different it would be without her dad there.

"Well," she said slowly. "My mom is pretty upset about the whole thing. She doesn't want to be alone in New York City. We moved there for my dad's job. It's not like she has a lot of close friends or family there."

"So would you and your mom move back to Paris too?" I asked.

"My mom doesn't want to go to Paris." She was quiet for a minute. "I told her I think we should move to Faraway. You know, like a *'trial'* move." Sophie paused. "She knows how much I liked it over the summer. Plus, it would be good for both of us to be around people who care about us."

I didn't say a word.

"So we're going to live at Gaga and my grandpa's house, at least for now. And I'm starting school with you in the fall. April, we're going to Faraway High together!" Her words bounced around and bumped into each other in my brain, like too many little kids on a trampoline.

I said the first thing that came to mind. "But what about your art school? You love it."

"Well, I'm kind of bummed about that." Sophie paused. "But how cool is it that we'll be going to school together?"

"Wow! It's like . . . going to be great!" I was fumbling. I knew that's how I felt—how I should feel—but I couldn't put my words together in a way that sounded good.

Sophie was quiet for a minute, like she was taking in my response. "Are you sure you think so?"

"Of course!" I said. "I'm really sorry about your parents, but I'm super excited you're moving to Faraway. I mean, I can't even believe it!"

It was the right thing to say, because when I finished, Sophie said she was glad I'm excited. "I have to go," she said. "But we'll talk soon." Then she laughed. "Soon we'll be talking all the time. How cool is that?"

"Very!" I said. Then we hung up, and I sat down on my bed. I'm still sitting here. I'm not even sure how long it has been. But when Sophie told me her news, it's like my brain split and went into two directions.

One part went right to thinking about Matt and how he's going to feel when Sophie's going to school with us this fall. He liked her. It would be hard for any boy not to. She's so cute and cool. He said we'd see how things are when school starts, but he didn't anticipate starting school with me *and* Sophie. Even though I'm starting to think maybe I'm better off without a boyfriend to worry about, I'd be lying if I didn't say that I'm more freaked out than ever about what's going to happen with Matt with Sophie in the picture.

But I hate myself for even thinking like that when Sophie just told me her parents are separating. She was there for me when Matt and I broke up. That was nothing compared to what she's going through. I need to be there for her now. And I want to be.

So I'm picking the other path. The path of possibility. Sophie is moving to Faraway! She's going to be my new almost-family best friend, and I honestly can't wait.

I hope Matt doesn't fall madly in love with Sophie. That would be weird in lots of ways. But I'm not going to think like that. As I told May earlier, it's easy to think the worst will happen, but it almost never does.

Bottom line: I'm ready to move forward. High school, here I come.

Ten Reasons My Life Is mostly Miserable

1. My mom: Flora.

2. My dad: Rex.

3. My little sister: May.

4. My baby sister: June.

5. My dog: Gilligan.

6. My town: Faraway, Alabama.

7. My nose: too big.

8. My butt: too small.

9. My boobs: uneven.

10. My mouth. Especially when it is talking to cute boys.

THE MOSTLY MISERABLE LIFE OF APRIL SINCLAIR

THE MOSTLY MISERABLE LIFE
OF APRIL SINCLAIR

Can You Say
Catastrophe?

LAURIE FRIEDMAN

THE MOSTLY MISERABLE LIFE
OF APRIL SINCLAIR

Too Good
to Be True

LAURIE FRIEDMAN

THE MOSTLY MISERABLE LIFE
OF APRIL SINCLAIR

Truth and Kisses

LET'S
KISS

FRIENDS
4EVER

TOO
SOON

MAYBE
NOT

LAURIE FRIEDMAN

THE MOSTLY MISERABLE LIFE
OF APRIL SINCLAIR

Love or
Something Like It

LAURIE FRIEDMAN

About the Author

Laurie Friedman has a lot in common with April Sinclair. She was the oldest of three girls, grew up in a small Southern town, and kept a journal in which she wrote about the excitement of falling in love for the first time and the heartache of breaking up. She remembers that time as being completely awful—but is grateful for all the material it gave her to write about.

Ms. Friedman is the author of the Mostly Miserable Life of April Sinclair series as well as the popular Mallory series and many picture books. A native Arkansan, she now lives in Miami, Florida, with her family and her adorable rescue dog, Riley. You can find Laurie B. Friedman on Facebook or visit her on the web at www.lauriebfriedman.com.